JOY

# JOY

*Original screenplay by*
**DAVID O. RUSSELL**

*Story by*
**ANNIE MUMOLO** *and* **DAVID O. RUSSELL**

FABER & FABER

First published in 2016
by Faber & Faber Limited
Bloomsbury House
74–77 Great Russell Street
London WC1B 3DA

Typeset by Country Setting, Kingsdown, Kent CT14 8ES
Printed in the UK by CPI Group (UK) Ltd, Croydon CRO 4YY

A CIP record for this book is available from the British Library

ISBN 978-0-571-33036-2

2 4 6 8 10 9 7 5 3

# Contents

# Introduction

Every story – for me to write it and film it – has to be inspired by passion and compassion for many, many, many, many things and souls and emotions and details and chances and darings within it. Above all, very specific people.

Here are the reasons I felt compelled to write this story and make this movie, as I can best express them here. Women characters, in their humanness and fierceness, became a critical inspiration in the previous three films: *The Fighter*, *Silver Linings Playbook*, and *American Hustle*. With *Joy* it goes a step farther, as the first film for me with the female protagonist at its heart and center. And several generations of women around her, all very distinct and different women: her mother, her grandmother, her sister, her best friend, her own daughter, her father's girlfriend, and the memory of Joy herself at age ten which haunts her in dreams and nightmares.

Inspired by numerous true stories, one in particular, as well imagined fiction, Joy is a seemingly ordinary person. But as with so many seemingly ordinary people, as in the three previous films, she became fascinating to me in the specific details of the very specific worlds and people she comes from and is made by. These include the people she loves, with their particular human ways, strengths, limitations, and heartbreaks. It also includes the magic and imagination of her childhood (the experience, the emotion, of joy, as a child). How the very existence of this childhood magic and joy will change and survive or die as this girl grows up and faces the world in all its unexpected turns, treacheries, and loyalties is the backbone of the story and why I wanted to make the movie. The magic, the joy, that must endure the compromises and disappointments of adult life, the exhaustion of having to earn a simple living, of taking a chance on love that ends in failed marriage and the overwhelming life of debt, bills, children, an entire family, depending on her – because like it or not, Joy was born to be, her Grandmother Mimi says, 'the unanxious presence in the room.' Mimi is herself this unanxious presence, the steadiest, most reliable presence, and believer, in Joy's life.

vii

Some are born to be this loyal one, to carry others on their shoulders, beginning in their childhoods. It is their nature. They cannot help it. They are loving and loyal and strong. But what of their own joy? Tracking the heartbeat of the magic or élan or love of life one knew and cherished as a child into the adult world can mean seeing that heartbeat grow so faint it can scarcely be heard, or maybe it disappears entirely. What has life become, then, at this point? Without music in it? How many times does one feel that life, and the love of life, are over, that one is dead, while still living? How many times can someone again, and again, relocate the song, the hope, the truly alive heartbeat worth living for, again? Is it possible?

Exactly how specific people are driven by, and must attempt to recreate and hold on to, a true love of life, to remain true to themselves in this way, is embedded in the core of the last three films I had the privilege to direct and write (or, in first case, at least did much writing on): *The Fighter, Silver Linings Playbook* and *American Hustle*. Each of these also had something and someone in it I felt I had known personally, either from the many worlds I saw and experienced growing up around New York, or had experienced or witnessed closely in my adult life. *Joy* is no different.

Her childhood world and life are defined by the father who runs a bus and truck auto body garage, an outspoken, expansive, romantic, intense man, whose business, like his marriage, was perpetually on the brink of falling apart, but who never fell out of love with being in love, which, oddly, will turn out to create *the* critical opportunity one day Joy needs at her lowest moment.

By contrast, Joy's mother is a quiet, solitary, childlike person, who withdrew from the world to her lovely simple room, where she finds solace and inspiration from the fierce women characters of *The Private Storm of Emily Rockman*, the soap opera she watches daily. And shows to her daughter, our heroine, from the early age of ten.

But Joy, as a child of ten on her own, seeks refuge in the world of her imagination, at a small table by the window in her room, where she crafts paper things with her hands, a paper house, a paper gate leading to a paper forest, where she narrates fables, where she can encounter and defeat dangers, one day, she imagines, to build a house of her own at the far end of the forest. She ritually tells, and plays out, this story in her paper forest, to herself, and for her older sister, while playing enchanting records, Prokofiev's *Cinderella*, to escape the explosive turmoil of the parents' marriage. The older sister is a watcher of Joy's enchantment rather than a creator of it, which naturally creates fascination, and also envy.

There is, in all of this, a great childhood love of snow. Which was fortunate because Boston had the greatest snowfall in its history during the exact months of our shoot there, January, February, March 2015, when a record shattering 110.6 inches fell, three inches more than the snowfall peak set twenty-one years before. Snow experienced as a child, and snow experienced as an adult, are the visual and emotional bookends of this cinematic story. The snow of Joy's adulthood, both at ages twenty-eight and forty-three, is replete with a seasoned life, a weathered joy, that has endured in a complex and mature fashion, that carries in it loyalty and heartbreak with equal acceptance.

In the 16 mm footage of Joy's childhood in the snow are seen some of the happiest moments Joy shares with her family, and also with her best friend, Jackie, with whom she sings songs. When they are eighteen, this best friend will take Joy to the party where Joy will meet the man who becomes her husband – a Venezualan singer in a family of singers, whose dream is to become the next Tom Jones. This man has tenderness, music, dreams, and, of course, zero practical ability to hold down a steady job as a provider, which quickly ends this marriage, as her father predicted, in turmoil and then divorce, as Joy cannot seem to avoid repeating the experience of her parents. With the one remarkable exception that also was something I felt I had not seen in a movie: the best divorced couple in America. They become best friends. Far better friends than marrieds. And he is happy and grateful to help Joy when she begins her endeavor as an inventor, and then to work for her, as his boss, serving her faithfully as a counselor and friend.

None of this had I seen before. All of it inspired me to write this movie, including the soap operas and the nightmares, from the ages of ten to forty-three, all things I had never done before. All in the most visually formal, composed design and camera approach by me and my devoted team of co-filmmakers, to use space, and light and shadow to define the aloneness, or smallness, or enchantment, or unexpected beauty, experienced by our heroine and those she encounters on her odyssey, as she goes from the world of her father and mother to the world of her husband then ex-husband to the world of the emerald city, the small cable station in Lancaster, Pennsylvania, where a man treats his new network that reaches into people's homes twenty-four hours a day, with the sincerity, seriousness of purpose and attention to detail and meticulousness and inspiration that some classic movie studio impresarios had for their enchantment factories in the forties and fifties.

In the end to find, and make, her own world, having arrived at last at her home, true to herself, through the journey and storm of it all. Much of the visual framing and design was inspired by films I love from the forties and fifties, as well as by the paintings and use of space and light of Edward Hopper and Andrew Wyeth. The ways in which these paintings locate the emotion of solitary individuals, in a crowd or alone, in ways that are somehow very beautiful, in spite of it all. Or maybe because of it all. These frames, as with creating the soap opera from black and white to color across four decades, were also important additional reasons and inspirations to make this film. And to impart throughout it all love, loyalty, maturity and poise in power, magic and hope, somehow, in spite of living through all the very real disappointments, compromises, and failures.

That's a movie I wanted to see. That felt worthy of asking for the privilege of again working with actors I have come to know and work with, as well as many new ones I have wanted to work with. I wrote this for them. Beginning with Jennifer. Jennifer most of all. And Robert. Robert. And Bradley. Bradley. By now, collaborators I am blessed to know. Then new collaborators: Edgar, Isabella, Diane, Virginia, Dasha. Then the youngest ones, Isabella, Madison, Andrea and Gia Gadsby. And the soap legends: Lucci, Mills, Bernard, Wright. And then all the many new discoveries in our cast. And for all the brave women I have known in my life, who got their chances or made the best with what they had, for better or worse, in strong ways: my mother, my ancestors, and so many others. Right up to Megan Ellison and Elizabeth Gabler, who have lived Joy in their very own lives.

David O. Russell
November 2015

# Cast and Crew

*Joy* was first released on 25 December 2015
A Twentieth Century Fox and Annapurna Picture presentation

### PRINCIPAL CAST

| | |
|---:|---|
| JOY | Jennifer Lawrence |
| RUDY | Robert De Niro |
| NEIL WALKER | Bradley Cooper |
| TONY MIRANDA | Edgar Ramirez |
| MIMI | Diane Ladd |
| TERRY | Virginia Madsen |
| TRUDY | Isabella Rossellini |
| JACKIE | Dascha Polanco |
| PEGGY | Elizabeth Rohm |
| DANICA | Susan Lucci |
| CLARINDA | Laura Wright |
| RIDGE | Maurice Benard |
| PRISCILLA | Donna Mills |

### PRINCIPAL CREW

| | |
|---:|---|
| *Directed by* | David O. Russell |
| *Screenplay by* | David O. Russell |
| *Story by* | Annie Mumolo, David O. Russell |
| *Produced by* | John Davis, Ken Mok, Megan Ellison |
| | Jonathan Gordon, David O. Russell |
| *Executive Produced by* | Matthew Budman |
| *Cinematography by* | Linus Sandgren |
| *Edited by* | Adam Baumgarten, Jay Cassidy |
| | Tom Cross, Christopher Tellefsen |
| *Music by* | West Dylan Thordson |
| | David Campbell, Blake Mills |
| *Production Design by* | Judy Becker |
| *Costume Design by* | Michael Wilkinson |
| *Casting by* | Mary Vernieu, Lindsay Graham |

# Joy

**THE SCREENPLAY**

*Magical bells play over opening logos, then lush warm orchestrated emotional score.*

INT. BLACK AND WHITE, DRAWING ROOM – DAY

*Soap opera from 1969, 'The Private Storm of Emily Rockman'.*
*Danica and Clarinda discuss Pendleton Industries.*

>                    CLARINDA
> It doesn't make sense. I don't understand how something like this happened, I don't know what I am going to do. This has been my whole life and now it's gone, I don't know what I am suppose to do. Pendleton Industries is all I've ever known and now it's all been taken away.

>                    DANICA
> When someone sees a weakness in me I turn the weakness into a strength.

*She pulls a gun, presents it to Clarinda.*

>                    CLARINDA
> Oh, Danica, you're so strong. I, I don't think I could ever do anything like this.

>                    DANICA
> You can imagine changing your life by fighting for the deed to the land, Clarinda. Which is only possible if Bartholomew is no longer living.

*Bartholomew enters the room.*

>                    BARTHOLOMEW
> You'll never get the deed to the land again, I will never allow it. Put down that gun, you silly girl.

>                    DANICA
> Watch your step, Bartholomew. Ridge is on his way and he is still in love with Clarinda, and Jared loves me.

RIDGE
Clarinda, it's true. I'm here for you.

*Cut to white letters on black. New percussive cue:*

INSPIRED BY TRUE DARING WOMEN

*Next card:*

ONE IN PARTICULAR

*Cut to:*

EXT. SNOW FALLS OVER SIMPLE CLAPBOARD HOUSE – DAY

GRANDMA MIMI
(*voice-over*)
This is the story of Joy. As told by me, her grandmother.

*Cut to:*

EXT. RUDY'S BUS AND TRUCK GARAGE – STILL SNOWING

*Camera pulls back through the big red rooftop letters:* RUDY'S BUS
AND TRUCK.

GRANDMA MIMI
(*voice-over*)
Everybody starts out with some kind of dream what life will be.
Joy's dream started at this metal garage that her father ran.

*Camera tilts directly down to see forty feet below empty frame of
white snow-covered ground as young Joy, ten, enters frame. Plays in
the snow. From high above we barely hear:*

YOUNG JOY
(*sings*)
Jackie, Jackie, bo backie, banana nana fo fackie, fe phi fo
fackie, Jackie.

GRANDMA MIMI
(*voice-over*)
My granddaughter had a best friend, Jackie –

*Young Jackie, Joy's best friend, runs into high wide shot.*

*Cut to:*

YOUNG JOY *and* JACKIE
(*sing together in snow*)
'While shivering in my shoes, I strike a careless pose, and
whistle a happy tune, so know one ever knows –'

*Cut to:*

*16 mm home movie: Young Joy and older sister Peggy play outside
Rudy's truck garage.*

GRANDMA MIMI
(*voice-over*)
A half-sister, Peggy –

*Cut to:*

*Young Joy concentrates on opening a small dog's collar in snow.*

GRANDMA MIMI
(*voice-over*)
A dog –

*Cut to:*

*16 mm. Rudy stands posed with family before large faded ad mural
of his face on side of truck garage.*

GRANDMA MIMI
(*voice-over*)
A father –

*Cut to:*

*16 mm. Joy's mother Terry, pretty, shy, gentle, waves to camera in
the snow.*

GRANDMA MIMI
(*voice-over*)
A mother –

*Grandma Mimi, vibrant, lively, confident, enters 16 mm, embraces
Terry.*

– who is my daughter.

GRANDMA MIMI
(*voice-over*)
A grandmother, that's me.

5

*Mimi blows kiss to 16 mm camera.*

INT. YOUNG JOY'S ROOM, 1969 – DAY

*Joy, ten, carefully stares through two stacked records on a 1969 child's record player. She places the needle down and 'Cinderella', by Prokofiev, plays.*

> GRANDMA MIMI
> (*voice-over*)
> Joy made many beautiful things in her room, magic. Some people love to make things. They have the patience and the focus to figure it out with their hands. Joy was one of those people who rejoiced in making things.

> YOUNG JOY
> (*narrates her created paper world*)
> And I opened the gate, to the big green meadow, and I went into the forest and there I conquered many dangers. A wolf and other scary things. And then I started to build my very own house, where I would live and make wonderful creations for all the world to see and have. Maybe for the prince and princess who lived across the forest in the castle, see. And they were in love.

> YOUNG PEGGY
> You need a handsome prince. That's what you need, a prince.

> YOUNG JOY
> No, I don't need a prince. This is a special power. (*Holds paper bird magically aloft.*) I don't need a prince.

*Cut to:*


INT. TERRY'S BEDROOM – DAY

*Terry sits, nicely dressed, on an empty white double bed.*

> GRANDMA MIMI
> (*voice-over*)
> My daughter is separated and alone in her room, watching her soap opera.

*Cut to:*

6

*Terry's television. Black-and-white 1969 soap opera plays.*

> DANICA
> You can imagine changing your life by fighting for the deed to the land, Clarinda. I have something for you.

> CLARINDA
> Oh, Danica, you're so strong, I don't think I could ever do something like this.

*Cut to:*

INT. TERRY'S BEDROOM – CONTINUOUS

*Young Joy now sits close watching soap opera on TV.*

> GRANDMA MIMI
> (*voice-over*)
> I always felt it was for me to encourage her, so I said –

INT. DOORWAY

*Young Joy faces silhouetted Grandma Mimi.*

> GRANDMA MIMI
> 'You are going to grow up and be a strong, smart young woman, go to school, meet a fine young man, have beautiful children of your own and you're going to build wonderful things like you do in your room.'

> GRANDMA MIMI
> (*voice-over*)
> What happened to this girl's dream? Watch this.

*Camera pans to black in closet, new percussive cue begins as camera pans back to reveal in silhouette twenty-seven-year-old Joy.*

> JOY
> Mother, I can't find my lanyard for work, they're not going to let me through airport security without it.

> GRANDMA MIMI
> (*voice-over*)
> Joy, you can't find your lanyard? Can I help you?

No, but I –

GRANDMA MIMI
(*voice-over*)

Honey, listen I know life hasn't gone the way we discussed many times, sweetheart, and you don't exactly have your whole life ahead of you, but you still have a good portion of it anyway. Hope brings eternal.

JOY

Thanks, Mimi.

*Mimi kisses Joy's cheek. Joy steps into light of Terry's room. She wears a navy Eastern Airline customer-service uniform, with neckerchief and vest.*

Mother, look what I did find.

*Terry, on bed watching soap, now seventeen years later, removes glasses to look at dog collar Joy holds out in one hand.*

TERRY

What's that?

JOY

How can you ask what this is? The dog collar I invented in high school. Remember Mitzy choked a couple of times so I invented a dog collar with a quick release so the dog would never choke and I covered it with reflective tape plus it's a flea collar. Now the Hartz Company has the patent to that collar.

TERRY

Joy the do-er, Joy the do-er, you were always doing so many things, how could I be expected to remember everything? I don't know how to get a patent.

JOY

What is that smell, ugh, how did you get yogurt down here, Mother?

TERRY

I was wondering what that odor was.

JOY

It's starting to mold, for Pete's sake.

*Cut to:*

*Terry's now-color television to see 1988 soap opera playing.*

CLARINDA
(*on TV*)
Yes, I am, because I feel like I can *not* have the life bled out of me this way.

*Cut to:*

TERRY
Joy, look who's back! Look who's back.

*Joy kneeling on floor to clean it, looks up at TV.*

*1988 soap opera on television: Sinister Bartholomew points at Clarinda.*

BARTHOLOMEW
Yes, Bartholomew is *back*.

JOY
I thought Bartholomew was dead.

TERRY
He came back as a ghost with even greater powers.

*Doorbell rings, Joy exits to answer, passing her children.*

JOY
Grandma's gonna take you to the birthday party okay, five minutes.

*Joy continues to the front door.*

EXT./INT. JOY'S EAST MEADOW HOUSE – DAY

*Joy opens the front door of the modest home, surprised to face her father, Rudy, sixty-five, sunglasses, dark wool topcoat, holding bundle of laundry under one arm and in other hand a suitcase. Behind him is Sharon, fifty-five, dark hair, pantsuit, tinted glasses. Joy stares.*

JOY
Hi. What are you doing here?

SHARON

I'm returning him to you, I don't want him anymore.

JOY

What?

SHARON

He's damaged. He has no place else to go, he's been in my house for two years.

JOY

Sharon, Dad, I'm sorry, but, you know, Tony's livin' in the basement.

RUDY

Your ex-husband shouldn't be living in your basement. That's not the proper way to be divorced.

JOY

Okay, but I don't know where I'm gonna put you.

*Rudy walks right past her with his suitcase.*

Dad, don't go in there, Mom's in there.

*Rudy is already past Joy with his suitcase and laundry.*

INT. TERRY'S BEDROOM – DAY – CONTINUOUS

*Terry's eyes widen as she sees her ex-husband walk in.*

SHARON

You can have him back, Terry. I don't want him anymore.

TERRY

What was so much better about being with Sharon, Rudy?

JOY

Dad, don't answer that.

RUDY

We went to the Metropolitan Museum of Art.

TERRY

What did you like at the Museum?

RUDY

What did I like, I'll tell you what I liked, I liked the ancient
Roman statues, I liked the medieval armor, I liked the Etruscan
jewelry, I liked going to the café, having an espresso, a nice
panini. That's what I liked.

TERRY

Museums are full of dust and death. You had a panini in a
coffin, Rudy. A dusty, boring, coffin, yuck.

RUDY

Then why did you ask me? What are you, a crazy person? It's
like having a conversation with an insane asylum person.

TERRY

What else, Captain Jack? What else was so great?

RUDY

Captain Jack? You call me Captain Jack?

TERRY

Yes, you're Captain Jack the Flying Jackass.

RUDY

You know what you are? You're like a gas leak. We don't smell
you, we don't see you but you're killing us all, silently.

TERRY

I am not a gas leak, you take that back, and tell me what else
you did with Sharon.

RUDY

You creature from the black lagoon.

JOY

This conversation is over.

SHARON

I'm leaving, good luck.

TERRY

Watch out, Joy, he's gonna snap, guard the china.

RUDY

You want me to snap, that's your routine, Terry, you like this,
how's this for snapping?

JOY

Dad, no!

*Rudy smashes a china figure to the floor.*

RUDY

How's this for snapping? Does this make you happy?

*Rudy clears bureau on to the floor.*

TERRY

He's disturbed, Joy. He's a disturbed man.

RUDY

I am disturbed. You're the great disturber.

*Rudy immediately walks to apologize to Joy, as Terry emotionally turns TV volume back up.*

I'm sorry, I'm gonna clean all this up.

JOY
(*carrying his suitcase*)
Stop, I'll do it, I just want to get you out of this room.

*Rudy hangs up the broken phone on floor.*

Thank you.

INT. HALL, LIVING ROOM – CONTINUOUS

*Joy leads Rudy to dining room where the door to the basement is, pauses to see her children, Christy and Tommy, with Grandma Mimi at dining table.*

JOY

Sorry about all the yelling, Mimi's gonna take you to the birthday party, okay?

RUDY

Hi, my sweethearts.

CHRISTY

You broke things again.

RUDY

I did break some things, but Grandma was wrong, so I was a little wrong but she was really wrong.

JOY

Grandpa's gonna come stay with us for a little while, isn't that nice?

EVERYONE

Yayyyy!

CHRISTY

A sleep-over with Grandpa! Yay!

RUDY
(sotto voce, gives laundry bundle to Joy)
Sharon never separated the wash. The whites were always gray, but you have that magic touch, sweetheart so can I –

Joy nods, takes laundry.

JOY

Yeah, I'll take care of it, just get your bag.

RUDY

What about the ledgers and all that stuff?

JUDY

I got that, I'll get them to you later.

CHRISTY

Love you, Grandpa.

RUDY

Love you.

INT. BASEMENT STAIRS – CONTINUOUS

Joy leads Rudy downstairs to the basement where he will stay.

JOY

I did your taxes, I did your W-2s.

INT. BASEMENT OF JOY AND TONY'S HOUSE – CONTINUOUS

Tony Miranda, thirty, Tom Jones bow tie undone, sings 'Waters of March' in Spanish, on vintage mic and amp, eyes closed, lost in his singing.

13

TONY
(*singing*)
'Esta noche' es la muerete es una zona es un arbol del campo
com nudo de madrea de la matita pereira flautas de.'

*Tony stops, stares at Rudy. They hate each other.*

What's he doing here?

JOY
(*puts laundry in machine*)
Sharon brought him back so he has to stay with us till he finds a
new love or a new place to live, you know how this goes.

TONY
(*in Spanish*)
'Yo no queiro a tu papa aqui.'

JOY
(*in Spanish*)
'Que' quieres que yo tengo que ir a trabajar.'

TONY
(*in Spanish*)
'Su padre es una pesadilla vamos a matarse unos a otros.'

JOY
(*in Spanish*)
'Yo no oir mas, es esto el punto.'

*With this, Joy closes the matter.*

TONY
(*in Spanish*)
Okay, but no me gusta, Joy, no me gusta.

JOY
Dad, up.

*Rudy stands from sofa as she converts it to a bed.*

RUDY
This is not the proper way to be divorced, the two of you.

TONY
You're gonna tell me how to be divorced?

RUDY

And I'm a provider, Tom Jones. I have my own business, I help Joy with the mortgage. What do you do? You sing all night at Angela Starpoli's club, you get repeatedly fired from Campbell's Soup.

JOY

Okay, well, I'm gonna divide the basement.

*Joy divides the basement in two with a roll of toilet paper.*

TONY

I'm divorced, Rudy, I can do whatever I want.

RUDY

This is not the proper way to be divorced.

JOY

I am about to be late for work so please try not to fight in front of the children, especially not physically.

*Tony points to his vintage microphone on the stand.*

TONY

Rudy you see this? You touch it, I kill you.

*Rudy stares down Tony without flinching.*

JOY

Please try not to kill each other while I'm gone.

*Goes back through house with Joy, past Terry watching the soap on TV. Follows Joy out the front door. She kicks at broken wood on her porch pillar.*

I thought I fixed this thing.

PEGGY
(*off-screen, shouts*)
Nice job, Joy, nice job!

JOY

Peggy?

*Cut to:*

*Pan reveals Peggy, Joy's older half-sister, shoulder-length hair, lumberjack coat, standing with truck at snowy driveway, as Mimi walks Joy's two small children out to the birthday party.*

15

PEGGY

I wasn't stupid enough to get into a bad marriage and have a couple of kids.

MIMI

Don't bother your sister, Peggy.

PEGGY

I'm here to talk to Dad about business, alright? You're gonna bring the books by the garage later?

JOY

Yeah, I'm going to bring them later. He's in the basement.

PEGGY

I'm joking with you. I'm joking with you.

JOY

Yeah, I know.

*Joy hurries to her car with her coffee mug in one hand and book-keeping stuff in the other.*

PEGGY

Kids, we're gonna do something fun later, okay.

MIMI

We're doin' somethin' fun now.

*Joy kicks and yanks her dented car door to open it with a creak.*

INT. EASTERN AIRLINES TICKET OFFICE – DAY

*Customer service chaos as Joy clicks computer keys.*

JOY

We found your luggage in Cleveland. So now we just need to get it back to New York City.

AIRLINE CUSTOMER
(*throws papers in Joy's face*)
I'm filing a complaint. My husband needs his medication. What's your name – Joy? You don't seem joyous to me today.

JOY

Perhaps I am not so joyous today.

CLERK 2

Joy, I think the supervisor wants to talk to you.

*Just then a Manager and Supervisor surround Joy.*

MANAGER

How you doin', listen, I need you to speak to the supervisor.

SUPERVISOR 2

We're gonna be having some changes and you're going to be going to the night hours and we're having cutbacks.

JOY

Tom, I can't work night hours, I have two kids.

CLERK 2

Sorry, Joy, good luck.

*Joy is led away as someone takes her place at the keyboard.*

EXT. RUDY'S GARAGE OFFICE – BODY SHOP – DAY

*Ella Fitzgerald's 'I Want to be Happy' plays as Joy walks toward Rudy's bus and truck garage where sparks fly as a school bus is welded out front.*

*Around the side of the garage, just on the other side of an old broken wood fence, is a makeshift gun range/junk yard.*

*BAM. A gun fires, shatters a bottle at the gun range. Joy covers her ears as she walks past the fence of the gun range on her left, and the faded mural of Rudy's garage on her right. She turns into the side garage opening.*

INT. RUDY'S GARAGE OFFICE – BODY SHOP – CONTINUOUS

*Joy walks past welding sparks and metal work inside the truck garage, to the upstairs office. Rudy on the phone.*

RUDY
(on office phone)

I'm not paying for metal that I haven't got, on top of which he wants to get paid, he doesn't send the metal then send an invoice, then I'll pay him. Yep, that's it, send the invoice.

*Rudy hangs up the phone as Joy takes ledgers out of her bag.*

17

JOY

Hi Dad, I want to thank you again for helping me again with
the mortgage. I settled the account and balanced the books. I'm
sorry business is so slow – do you think it has anything to do
with the crazy gun range that's right next door? I mean, how is
that even legal, it's been there twenty years, doesn't it bother you?

RUDY

They keep to themselves, it's not my property, the police leave
them alone, do you think it's costing us business?

JOY

I don't think it's helping.

PEGGY
(*walks in*)

Well, if you want to help why don't you come here and manage
this place, I'd like to go to the next level, put on a nice suit, go
out there and get some accounts.

*Rudy, dialling the phone, holds his hand up to shush his daughters.*

RUDY
(*on phone*)

Shhh. (*Now into phone.*) Yes, this is 9873, just checking my
mailbox.

*Joy observes her father, puzzled.*

JOY

What is that?

RUDY
(*phone to ear*)

Yeah, I have a pen, what is it? 1314, that's it. Thank you.

JOY

What was that?

RUDY
(*hesitant*)

It's a 900 number.

JOY

What's a 900 number?

RUDY

It's, you know, a dating service. For widows and widowers.

JOY

You're not a widow or a widower.

RUDY

What's the difference, I'm single, I meet nice ladies, maybe we fall in love. I have to fall in love or I'm not interested. You know me.

JOY

I know, Dad –

RUDY

Shhhh.

PEGGY
(*whisper*)

Sharon was no good for him, it's nice for him to meet somebody new. I got him some new clothes, you know.

JOY

Okay, okay, it's good.

PEGGY
(*kisses Joy's cheek*)

Love you, see you later.

*Joy continues to watch her father on his dating phone call.*

RUDY
(*on phone*)

Hello, is this 7633?

TRUDY
(*off-screen, on phone*)

Yes.

RUDY
(*shy, on phone*)

Hi, this is 9833.

TRUDY
(*off-screen*)

Oh! Hi. How are you?

RUDY

What a nice voice you have.

TRUDY

Thank you.

RUDY

Oh, an accent.

*Cut to:*

*Wide shot. Trudy sits elegantly dressed, Italian, far side of elegant large room.*

TRUDY

Oh, yes I am from Italy.

RUDY
*(off-screen, on phone)*

Oh, continental.

*Back to Rudy on phone at metal garage.*

TRUDY
*(off-screen, on phone)*

What is your name?

RUDY

My name is Rudy, what's yours?

TRUDY
*(off-screen, on phone)*

Trudy.

RUDY

Are you kidding me. Your name is Trudy.

TRUDY
*(off-screen, laughs)*

Yes.

RUDY

Rudy and Trudy. I love it. Let's, let's figure out when we are going to meet.

TRUDY
*(off-screen, on phone)*
That's a good idea, let's have dinner. I will come and pick you up. I have a green Mercedes.

RUDY
Okay, six-thirty, I'll be ready.

TRUDY
*(off-screen)*
Ciao.

*Rudy hangs up, all aglow with new romance.*

JOY
Good luck with your date, Dad.

RUDY
Thank you, I'm excited.

JOY
What do you think you're gonna wear?

INT. JOY AND TONY'S HOUSE – NIGHT

*Basement door opens, Rudy presents himself.*

RUDY
*(posing)*
Polo, by Ralph Lauren.

*For his date: pink Oxford shirt, yellow polo sweater, light-tan blazer and slacks.*

TONY
*(holds three-year-old Tommy)*
Did you use the whole bottle of cologne? Huh?

JOY
Tony.

TONY
You smell like my grandmother. He smells like my grandmother.

**RUDY**

Now please, don't make me tense. Don't stress me out. I gotta stay nice and loose.

**TONY**

Ah, you're tense?

**RUDY**

I'm tense, you're making me tense.

**JOY**

Guys, stop.

**TONY**

Yeah, I'm making you tense.

**JOY**

Please.

**RUDY**

Gotta stay loose for the big date.

*Car horn beeps outside.*

My carriage awaits meeee.

**JOY**
(*hugs her father*)

Have a great date.

**RUDY**

Wish me luck.

**JOY**

You don't need it.

*Joy now stands alone, stressed as the household continues to call upon her from all directions: off-screen, Christy yelling from upstairs, Tony from the kitchen.*

**TONY**
(*off-screen*)

And where are my cufflinks?

**CHRISTY**
(*off-screen*)

Mommy, come read to me.

JOY

Five minutes, Christy.

TERRY

Joy, water!

JOY

Mother again.

INT. TERRY'S BEDROOM

*Joy walks into her mother's room, enveloped by the music of the soap on TV, as Terry and three-year-old Tommy sit in TV's light as Terry points at water coming out of the floor. Joy enters and flips up the waterlogged carpet.*

JOY

Yeah, you just sit right there. Are you comfortable?

*Joy takes mallet, chisel, and prises open floor boards. Water sprays from leaking pipe as Joy tightens valve with wrench –*

JOY
(*fixing pipe*)

How many times do I have to tell you not to clean your brushes out in the sink?

TERRY

Danica thinks it's unladylike to toss things in the toilet, and I happen to agree.

JOY

Yeah, well, why don't you have Danica do your plumbing then, huh?

*Terry's TV with Danica's scene.*

DANICA
(*on TV*)

Danica can direct her power anywhere Danica chooses. *That* is the power of Danica.

JOY
(*shutting off floor pipe*)

If this problem gets any worse we're gonna have to move you

into a different room. That means no TV. It could be very scary for you.

*Terry looks mortified from her bed.*

TERRY

Don't let that happen, Joy, this room is my comfort nest –

JOY

We're gonna need to get a plumber in here.

TERRY

*What?* A man . . . in my room?

JOY

I don't know any female plumbers, other than me.

TERRY

Well, can't you fix it, Joy?


INT. LIVING ROOM – NIGHT

*Christy lies in Joy's arms while sitting on the couch. Joy is reading a book about cicadas to her.*

JOY
(*reading children's book*)
'The cicada is a large flying insect two to three inches long, it makes a sound of up to 120 decibels, louder than some telephones. It lives half of its life above ground evading predators.' This is the book you wanted me to read to you, Christy? How did this book even get in the house?

CHRISTY

Aunt Peggy got it for me. She said the reason I like cicadas because they fill the air with sound which makes the house less lonelier for me.

JOY

Aunt Peggy tells you how *you* feel about the house being lonely?

CHRISTY

Aunt Peggy tells me a lot of things. Keep reading, please.

JOY
(*stares at Christy*)
I don't want you listening to Aunt Peggy too much.

CHRISTY
Okay. Why?

JOY
(*sighs, keeps reading*)
'The cicada, a symbol of rebirth in many countries, digs into the
ground and stays buried for up to seventeen years.' That's such
a random number, why seventeen years? It doesn't even say
*why*? I understand the four seasons in a year, but why would
something stay hidden for seventeen years. That's just unsettling.
I'm not reading this, you're sleepy anyway, we got to go to bed.

*Joy and Christy get up and head upstairs.*

CHRISTY
I want to sleep with Nanna.

JOY
No, you should sleep upstairs in your room.

CHRISTY
I want Nanna.

JOY
(*picks up Christy*)
Watch out, there is a hole in the floor here.

*Joy puts the kids to sleep. Joy's eyes flutter closed. Joy sleeps. Push in
on Joy sleeping. Soap drones on TV, crosses into flickering dimness or
just into the TV and on to the set of the soap.*

I'm just going to lay down for a second. I feel like I'm in a prison.

TERRY
No, Bartholomew is the ex-con in this story and Clarinda
doesn't even know about it. Danica's on to him.

*Camera moves across Joy's face as she lies sleeping on the bed,
toward the color television screen – into the soap that is playing with
Susan Lucci (Danica), Laura Wright (Clarinda), Maurice Bernard
(Ridge), Donna Mills (Priscilla).*

INT. TERRY'S BEDROOM – CONTINUOUS

*Soap opera plays on TV.*

BARTHOLOMEW
No, it wasn't because of me, it was because of Clarinda.

CLARINDA
No, no.

PRISCILLA
Yes, it was you, Clarinda.

DANICA
I will get to the bottom of this.

PRISCILLA
You've made terrible mistakes.

BARTHOLOMEW
It was Clarinda.

INT. SOAP OPERA MANSION

*Everyone's attention is drawn to Joy, who appears in the soap opera. A wave of escalating orchestra lands in sudden silence.*

BARTHOLOMEW
Oh.

DANICA
Look who's here.

CLARINDA
Look who's here.

BARTHOLOMEW
Look who's here.

*Cut to:*

INT. SOAP OPERA MANSION – JOY'S NIGHTMARE

*Joy stands confused and scared facing the soap characters in the soap opera mansion. Her father, ex-husband, and sister, in glamorous soap attire, walk towards her. Peggy carries chloroform, pours it into a*

*napkin, covers Joy's mouth with it as she tries to turn away.*
*Orchestra swells again, as suddenly –*

INT. BACKSEAT OF A CAR

*Joy jerks back as car takes off; her father and Peggy sit on either side*
*of her. Suddenly she is in a beautiful church with light streaming in*
*the windows and choir singing, as –*

EXT./INT. SOAP OPERA CATHEDRAL

*Joy walks with her family through pools of light and shadow up the*
*centre aisle of the church to the singing chorus till she sits, with*
*Rudy, Terry, Peggy, in the first two pews at a service – what kind of*
*service? Joy sees childhood picture of herself at the altar: it is a*
*funeral.*

> YOUNG JOY
> (*voice-over*)
> Do you remember that day seventeen years ago?

*Chorus continues as memory begins of Joy in her room with her*
*paper creations and her sister, seventeen years ago. Rudy and Terry*
*burst in, mid-argument. As Joy and her sister turn around scared, she*
*sweeps her creations into her shoebox.*

> YOUNGER RUDY
> Peggy comes with me, Joy spends half the time here, half the
> time with us.

*He reaches for Joy's box of creations to claim it. Terry grabs Joy's*
*shoebox to keep it in the house, Terry and Rudy fight for it, the box*
*is torn and falls to the floor. Joy, ten, cries, as does her sister. Rudy*
*kneels to hug Joy and apologize.*

INT. TERRY'S BEDROOM, JOY'S HOUSE – SAME NIGHT

*Joy awakes in the darkness from her troubling dream and memory.*
*TV still playing.*

> TERRY
> Joy, wake up. Someone's ringing the doorbell.

*Joy gets up, disoriented and disturbed by the dream.*

INT. JOY'S HOUSE HALLWAY/FRONT DOOR – CONTINUOUS

*Joy walks to the door, opens it: Jackie, Joy's friend since childhood.*

> JOY
> Jackie! Oh my God! It's you.

> JACKIE
> What happened? I'm worried about you. I don't see you
> anymore. You don't come to P.T.A.

INT. JOY'S KITCHEN – NIGHT

*Joy sits at kitchen table with Jackie.*

> JOY
> You know how my mom's always clogging the sink with her
> hair from the brushes.

> JACKIE
> With the pipes in her room.

> JOY
> Yeah, she did it again.

> JACKIE
> Again.

> JOY
> Yes and I had to bash open a hole in the floor, there's a huge
> hole in the floor, in my mother's room. And I'm broke. My
> father works hard, he's had some bad breaks, but I hope he gets
> another girlfriend and moves out of the basement.

> JACKIE
> He's in the basement with Tony?

> JOY
> Yes, and they hate each other.

> JACKIE
> Yes.

> JOY
> It's a disaster, they won't stop fighting. I don't know, how are
> you, how's the family, how is everybody?

28

JACKIE

Everybody is okay.

JOY

How's work?

JACKIE

My job, I can take it or leave it.

JOY

What happened to us, Jackie? All the things that we used to
dream about I feel like they keep getting further and further away.

JACKIE

Remember the night of that party, when we were eighteen, we
were so excited about everything –

*Memory of the past, party music, fades up on Joy's face as she
remembers.*

*Cut to:*

INT. MUSIC CONTINUES

*We see silhouettes of Joy at eighteen and Mimi, younger, at closet
door of Terry's room*

GRANDMA MIMI
(*voice-over*)

Honey, you're almost nineteen, you can't stay in your room all
the time working on whatever projects: your dog collar this,
your gripping hanger that. You got to get out, sweetheart, and
meet people. That's why I want you to go to that party tonight.

JOY

I'm not gonna know anybody there.

TERRY

Joy, there's water coming out of the wall.

*Joy reaches under Terry's bed, pulls out old wrench, bashes out a
neat box of old dry wall, a pipe trickles with a leak as Joy reaches
inside wall with wrench.*

If you think and talk like Danica there is no one and nothing
that you can't handle. So you can handle that party.

INT. TONY MIRANDA'S FAMILY HOME – NIGHT

*Door opens into a college party in a teacher's home. Reveal Joy's childhood friend Jackie, now eighteen, with Andre, twenty, African American.*

JACKIE

Joy!

JOY

Hi!

JACKIE

I'm so glad you came, this is my boyfriend, Andre.

JOY

Hi, Andre.

ANDRE

Nice to meet you.

JACKIE

Andre, this is my childhood friend Joy. Come inside.

*Jackie brings Joy inside the party. A Latin band plays, people dance.*

This is my music class.

JOY

This is a class?

JACKIE

Yes.

*Joy and Jackie watch Tony as he sings with his father:*

TONY
(*sings with his father*)
'Mama told me not to come. / Mama told me not to come. / She said / That ain't the way to have funnn / sonnnn.'

JOY

Who's the bald guy?

JACKIE

That's my music teacher, it's his house. He's from Venezuela.

30

JOY

Who's the guy singing with him?

JACKIE

That's the music teacher's son.

*Cut to:*

*Tony teaches an exuberant Joy the cha-cha – twirls her as they dance until, on the beat, Tony leads her right out of the living room towards a nested quiet corridor.*

JOY

What am I doing now?

TONY

You're dancing. Let me show you my father's stuff.

JOY

What?! What?!

INT. HALLWAY – CONTINUOUS

TONY
(*happy, pulling her along*)

Yeah yeah yeah.

*They settle in front of a bulletin board filled with sheet music.*

I'm going to be a singer.

JOY

Really.

TONY

Yes, I going to be the next Tom Jones.

JOY

Well, that's a big ambition, there's only one Tom Jones.

TONY

I know, but you can't let the practical get you down. You gotta keep going to what you love.

JOY

That's true.

31

TONY

That's what my father taught me. (*He pauses.*) What about you?

JOY

I invented a dog collar and I want to get patent but I don't think it ever will. Umm, I was valedictorian in high school. I got into a college in Boston but I, um, stayed here because my parents are getting divorced, I had to help my mom and I help my dad with business stuff, accountant.

TONY

Maybe your dreams are on hold for now.

JOY

That's a nice way of putting it.

*Both staring at each other, falling for each other, until Tony pulls lyrics from his father's bulletin board.*

TONY

This is the song my father is teaching right now in his class.

*Tony reads the sheet music and tries to get Joy to sing along with him: 'Somethin' Stupid'.*

TONY
(*sings*

'I know I'll stand in line / Until you think you have the time / To spend an evening with me.'

JOY

That's really nice.

TONY

Okay, go.

JOY
(*giggles*)

No.

TONY *and* JOY
(*sing gently together*)

'And if you go some place to dance, / I know that there's a chance / You wont be leaving with me.'

GRANDMA MIMI
(*voice-over*)
He gave my girl a spring in her step just when she needed it.

*Cut to:*

*Backstage, Joy and Tony's school musical (music playing in the background).*

GRANDMA MIMI
(*voice-over*)
He got her to do the college musical, something she never would have done.

*Music plays. Tony walks on to a stage as it snows and begins to sing to Joy.*

TONY
(*sings*)
'I know I'll stand in line / Until you think you have the time / To spend an evening with me. / And if we go some place to dance / I know that there's a chance / You won't be leaving with me.'

*Joy walks into the snow on stage toward Tony.*

JOY
(*sings*)
'And afterwards we drop into / A quiet little place and have a drink or two. / And then I go and spoil it all / by saying something stupid like I love you.'

TONY AND JOY
(*sing*)
'I can see it in your eyes / That you despise / The same old lies / You heard the night before.'

*Cut to:*


INT. FOYER OF CHURCH – JOY'S WEDDING DAY –1982

*In soft, natural back light, Rudy and Joy stand and face each other in silent suspense, both dressed in white for the wedding. Rudy speaks quietly.*

RUDY

You're so smart, you're so beautiful, you coulda married anybody, an actor, a lawyer, a nice man, instead of this, I don't even know what to call this guy.

JOY

Are you seriously talking about this right now?

*He pulls the white veil over her face.*

RUDY

It's not too late.

JOY

Dad.

PEGGY

Let's go.

*They walk to the entrance to the church. Rudy pauses one more time with Joy on his arm, looks at her.*

RUDY

Think about it.

JOY

Dad.

*She pulls him ahead into the church.*

*Cut to 16 mm:*

*Family posing post-wedding at reception – to Willie West, 'Baby I Love You'. Joy looks very happy, as does everyone, very, very happy and laughing and giddy as they cut the cake, pose for pictures, dance in a big circle. Everyone is in white.*

*Cut to:*

INT. LARGE BANQUET HALL

*Many tables – at the head table sit both families, left to right.*

*Tony's father, the singer we first saw when she met Tony, stands giving his sincere toast:*

TONY'S FATHER

We are a loving family, a solid family, I have been married to my wife –

*A clinking glass, ding-ding-ding, interrupts this toast – turns the crowd to Rudy, feeling the champagne as he stands, raising his glass. Joy looks up, seated by Rudy.*

RUDY

Now I have a speech.

JOY

He wasn't finished, Dad.

RUDY

He's finished now. I had two failed marriages. The daughter from my first marriage, Peggy, has a lot of tension with the daughter from my second marriage, Joy. I was married to Joy's mother for eighteen miserable fucking years.

*Terry shields her eyes in embarrassment as room quietly gasps. Mimi stares in shock next to Terry.*

*Joy yanks at Rudy's white tux sleeve.*

JOY

Dad, stop, that's just mean, sit down.

RUDY

But I got out of all that and finally met the light of my life, Sharon. To you, baby!

SHARON
(*raises her glass*)

You're my guy.

RUDY

I toast to you.

JOY

Dad, stop, you stop it right now.

*Joy jerks Rudy down by his tux, smashing him shoulder first to the table in a clatter of plates, glasses, and silver. People react quietly throughout the room. Tony leans down to Rudy angrily.*

TONY

Are you happy?

RUDY

No, not too happy.

*Rudy stands again, salad all over the shoulder and arm of his white tux, to now raise a broken champagne flute.*

Look what I found: the Divorce Glass. I give these kids fifty-fifty odds.

JOY

Dad!

RUDY

Enjoy, everybody, have a good time.

INT. JOY'S MODEST HOUSE, FIVE YEARS LATER (1987) – DAY

*Bee Gees, 'To Love Somebody', begins full as –*

*Joy, twenty-five, towel around her wet hair, carries screaming baby Tommy as she gives an alibi to Tony's boss on the phone while she tries to fill a baby bottle with milk. She passes Christy, three, making a mess in a corner of the kitchen.*

JOY

Oh, Christy, what are you doin' honey. (*Now calls to next room.*) Tony get up, Christy hasn't eaten, Tommy needs to be changed.

*Joy wears her airline service-desk uniform as she extends the kitchen phone cord thirty feet to the disheveled living room, where Tony lies on the sofa hungover in a tux from last night's singing, bandaged cut on his forehead.*

Get up, I just told your boss that you were going to work. You're going to lose another job.

TONY

No, honey, I'm sick –

JOY

You're not sick, you're hungover.

36

TONY

That's not who I am. I'm a singer, that's what I do.

JOY

You're not making any money singing. Get in your car right
now and go to your job.

TONY

You're trying to turn me into someone I'm not.

JOY

I can't do this! I can't do this, Tony! I am losing my mind!

*Tony starts to cry, Joy starts to cry.*

I don't want to end up like my family.


INT. LAWYER'S OFFICE – DAY

*Close up: Joy signs divorce decree. Pull out to her and Tony in
silhouette. Bee Gees, 'To Love Somebody', continues, fades.*

*Cut back to:*

*Joy and Jackie sit at kitchen table, silently facing what their lives
have become since they were kids. Tea kettle boils and we hear
Rudy's hearty laughter as:*

*Camera pulls out from Joy and Jackie at the kitchen table.*

*Cut to:*


EXT. JOY'S HOUSE – NIGHT

*Motor of a green Mercedes runs in the driveway.*


INT. TRUDY'S GREEN MERCEDES – CONTINUOUS

*Trudy the elegant Italian widow, Rudy's 900-number date, is giddy
with fun after dinner and drinks, laughing joyously with Rudy in his
'Polo by Ralph Lauren' style. They are aglow with romance, life,
love.*

TRUDY

Do I live up to my profile or do I fall short?

RUDY

Are you kidding? You're a banana flambé with extra rum, a trip
to the moon on gossamer wings.

TRUDY

(*laughs ecstatically*)

Oh wow! You're so poetic and romantic. Oh, just like my late
Morris.

RUDY

Morris, now he was American and you are Italian and your
name originated how?

TRUDY

Oh, my name. My Italian name is Gertrude. Then he called me
Trude. And then it became more American, Trudy.

RUDY

(*smiles*)

Trudy.

TRUDY

Why don't you come with your entire family on my late Morris'
boat. Bring the children, bring the grandchildren.

RUDY

Like a motor boat?

TRUDY

No, it's a sail boat, fifty-five feet.

RUDY

Oh wow, that's big. That is big. I would love to, we bring some
nice food and something to drink.

TRUDY

Yes, but not red wine, because it might stain the teak wood
deck, it's very precious.

RUDY

Okay, understood, no red wine.


EXT. MARINA DOCK – SUNNY WINTER DAY

*Trudy's impressively large sailboat.*

I got red wine!

*He carries a case of wine in his arms towards the gangplank. Trudy,
Rudy, Joy, her kids, Tommy and Christy, and Peggy, look at him
from the boat, all dressed in winter coats and hats.*

TRUDY

No, no, I'm sorry, you can't have red wine on the boat.

RUDY

No red wine, Tony. No red wine.

TONY

Why? It's a beautiful wine.

RUDY

What's Tom Jones doing here anyway? Who invited him?

JOY

He's here to help me with the kids.

RUDY

That's why I brought Peggy to help.

JOY

Peggy says mean things about me to my children.

PEGGY

I say nice things too.

TONY

It's a beautiful wine.

TRUDY

You have an accent too, where you from, paisano?

RUDY

Paisano – don't encourage him, please.

TONY

I'm from Venezuela, darling. Do you know this song?

*Sings same song he sang in basement, 'The Waters of March'.*

'Un palo, una piedra –'

*Trudy, giddy, sings each line after he does.*

                    TRUDY
                   (*sings*)
'Un palo, una piedra –'

                     TONY
                    (*sings*)
'Es el final del camino
Que es el resto del muñón
Que es un poco solos
Es una astilla de vidrio
Que es la vida, es el sol.'

                    TRUDY
I can see why she still loves him. C'mon, come on board.

                     RUDY
Oh this is gonna be a disaster.

*Cut to:*

*Tony pouring red wine into the wine glasses everyone holds.*

                      JOY
I dressed for boating but I didn't realize how cold it was going
to be.

                    TRUDY
My late husband Morris: I met him in Milan for a trade show
for his swimwear line. He used to say, 'Sailing in winter is the
best comparison to life in the world of commerce.'

*People laugh as Joy listens. The boat shoves off, operated by Trudy's
crew member. Sinatra's 'The Good Life' comes on full.*


EXT. BOAT DECK – DAY – LATER

*The beautiful sailboat, named 'The Morris', cuts through the water
on this sunny day, until a swell violently rocks the boat, throwing
everyone to their seats, wine glasses in hands. When the boat jolts the
opposite way, Joy and others are flung from their seats to the deck.*

*Wine glasses and red wine crash to the deck. Joy looks horrified.*

                    TRUDY
Oh no, Morris' teak-wood deck.

RUDY

Yeah, grand adventure, nice work, Tom Jones.


EXT. BOAT BACK AT THE DOCK – LATER

*Trudy laughs with Rudy, Peggy, Tony, in the background as Joy mops broken glass and red wine with an old string mop which she wrings with her hands.*

TONY

Trudy, I know it's upsetting, but wouldn't Morris say what a grand adventure?

TRUDY

You're right, no big deal, he's probably laughing up in heaven.

PEGGY

We should have used paper cups.

TONY

It's not the same, you need a nice glass for a beautiful wine, you know.

*Joy looks at the glass, cutting her hands as she wrings the mop. Match cut to:*


INT. JOY'S HOUSE – NIGHT

*Joy's hands as Mimi and Tony remove glass with tweezers and apply a bandage to one hand. Joy is lost in reverie, murmuring to herself.*

GRANDMA MIMI
(*voice-over*)

It's a piece of glass right in her hand.

TONY

Are you alright, honey? (*With concern as Joy stands.*) Are you alright?

*Joy whispers to herself, thinking of something in her head. It seems a little odd, but she has become a bit unhinged from all the stress and mishaps, and is now caught up in a reverie in her mind.*

GRANDMA MIMI
(*voice-over*)

She's thinking of something.

RUDY

It's strange. Honey, you should go to bed.

JOY
(*thinking*)

Shhh. It would all have to be one continuous loop, wouldn't it?

*Doorbell rings. Joy goes to answer door.*

*Cut to:*

*Joy opens door to reveal a handsome Haitian working man.*

TOUSSAINT

Hi, I am Toussaint.

RUDY

Toussaint? Who's this guy?

*Joy doesn't know. She turns around perplexed, looks at Rudy and Tony.*

It's not for me, is it for you?

TONY

It's not for me.

*Joy suddenly remembers.*

JOY

Oh, the plumber.

*She welcomes Toussaint inside.*

RUDY

What's he here for?

JOY

What do you think? Terry.

*She leads Toussaint to Terry's room.*

RUDY

Terry, ah Terry.

*Joy and Toussaint enter Terry's room, engulfed as always in lush soap opera score and the gentle blue light of the television in the dimness. Terry is taken aback. She sits up in her clothes on the bed.*

TERRY

Oh, no, what's going on? What's this man doing in my room?

JOY

This is –

TOUSSAINT

Toussaint.

JOY

Toussaint. Terry, Toussaint. Remember the plumber you need in here?

TERRY

Well, I, I taped my show and then, well, exactly how long is this going to take?

*She stands and, flustered and mildly irritated, gathers her magazines and coffee cup.*

TOUSSAINT

It shouldn't take more then a day.

TERRY

What is that accent, Joy? What country is that from?

TOUSSAINT

Haiti.

TERRY

Haiti.

TOUSSAINT

It's French and Creole.

JOY

French and Creole.

TERRY

Is there any way could you please put up a curtain here so that I can come and go in my room and watch my show while he's still working.

TOUSSAINT

Of course.

*Joy and Toussaint proceed to staple a drop-cloth curtain to divide Terry's room.*

TERRY

Thank you, sir.

TOUSSAINT

You're welcome, mademoiselle.

TERRY
(*as curtain blocks her*)

Mademoiselle?

*Joy exits Terry's room and heads towards the stairs.*

JOY

Good luck in here and good luck with that.

*She pauses halfway up the stairs.*

RUDY

Why don't you go to bed, keep going up the stairs. Go to bed.

JOY

I don't want to go to sleep, I don't want to have that horrible dream.

RUDY

Come on, you can't have the same dream twice. It never happens. It's impossible.

JOY

That's not true, I had the Peggy dream so many times when I was younger, with the mask and the ropes.

RUDY

You can't have the same dream twice.

GRANDMA MIMI
(*voice-over*)

Rudy, she's thinking of something.

TONY

Maybe it's a good dream and she is working something out.

JOY

I don't want to work anything out, I just want a nice dumb sleep.

44

RUDY

Let's knock her out, give her some children's cough medicine.
That's what does it.

*Rudy walks off to get the cough medicine.*

TONY

What? Is that safe?

GRANDMA MIMI
(*voice-over*)

No, it's not safe.

*Tony takes the cough medicine from Rudy's hand and reads it.*

TONY

It's expired.

*Rudy and Tony pour Joy children's cough medicine as she sits on the
carpeted stairs.*

RUDY

Go on there, knock it back, honey.

GRANDMA MIMI
(*voice-over*)

No.

RUDY

Okay, one more, knock it down. Come on.

TONY

Rudy!

JOY

Do it, Tony.

RUDY

Come on, just do it one more.

GRANDMA MIMI
(*voice-over*)

Rudy.

GRANDMA MIMI

Okay, enough of this. I'm going to make her a hot toddy, that's
what she needs.

*Cut to:*

*Close on the soap opera on Terry's TV.*

DANICA
I was kidnapped by another monk who was from Switzerland
and it turned out that this monk was a duke of a royal family.

*Back to:*

JOY
(*mutters, asleep on stairs*)
Leave me alone.

*Rudy and Tony look at Joy dozing on the stairs.*

RUDY
I don't think we should let her sleep on the stairs.

*Cut to:*

*Rudy and Tony carry Joy gently to the sofa and set her down. Rudy
kisses her forehead as she sleeps, with bandages on one hand.*

*On Joy's face. A muted doorbell rings, a door opens –*

*Back to another dream for Joy – in the soap opera mansion, as she,
Tony, Rudy, Trudy, Peggy, Terry, await who is at the door.*

YOUNG JOY
(*off-screen*)
You all thought I was dead, didn't you?

*The dream reveals it is young Joy, at ten years old, who has entered
the mansion and now speaks with authority and insight.*

YOUNG JOY
Did you say it made no sense for something to hide for
seventeen years? We've been hidden for seventeen years. What
have you been doing? We used to make things.

*Joy listens and stares, riveted, unsettled, at herself when she was ten,
as young Joy approaches her intensely.*

When you're hiding you're safe because people can't see you.
But funny thing about hiding, you're even hidden from yourself.

*Joy stares at herself as a girl, now facing her at point-blank range,
having accused Joy of hiding for seventeen years.*

46

*Cut to:*

EXT. JOY'S HOUSE – MORNING NEXT DAY

*Church bell rings in distance.*

INT. JOY'S HOUSE – CONTINUOUS

*Joy wakes up on the couch, observed by Tony and Rudy. She stares at them, a very different, serious look on her face.*

> TONY

What's the matter?

> JOY

Tony, you need to move out of the basement. You need to get your own house.

> TONY

What, why? Because I go out at night and sing at Angela's Club?

> JOY

No. Because we've been divorced for two years, we need to move on. You need to move out.

*She turns to Rudy.*

Rudy you need to move out too.

> RUDY

Why? There's more room in the basement for me now.

> JOY

And another thing, Rudy, tomorrow I would like to have a meeting with you and Trudy at your office to discuss her investing in the manufacturing of my new idea.

> RUDY

No. I'm still getting to know her. I'm falling in love. I can't do that, I won't do that. And what manufacturing idea? What are you talking about?

> JOY

I have always been there for whatever you needed, no matter what. I stayed to help Mom through the divorce, all your

47

bookkeeping, you stay here whenever you've wanted. I am respectfully asking for the favor that you owe me. If you look in your heart you know I'm right.

*Rudy stares at Joy, he knows she's right. Joy turns to Christy.*

Christy, I need to use your crayons, your color pencils, and your paper.

CHRISTY

Let's go to my room.


INT. CHRISTY'S ROOM – DAY

*Joy sits at what was once her childhood table but now is Christy's. She uses Christy's crayons to draw circles and shapes, putting to paper the idea she sees in her mind, since she first envisioned it the previous night. Christy watches, as does Mimi, seated in a small chair at the table. Joy takes a doll's looped hair, studies the loops closely, as she got lost in her paper creations as a child.*

*Joy then places all her drawings which appear to be a blueprint of something and tapes them on the wall. Christy and Grandma Mimi watch Joy as she studies the drawings.*


EXT. RUDY'S GARAGE – DAY

*Joy holds Christy's hand in one arm and her drawings in the other as she walks, with Jackie, past the gun range covering Christy's ear.*

JOY

You're not going to believe this, so you know that plumber you recommended?

JACKIE

Umm hmm.

JOY

So I hire him, Terry freaks out, completely disoriented, hasn't had a man in her room for eight years since Rudy. Makes me hang a drop-cloth.

48

INT. MAIN OFFICE – RUDY'S TRUCK AUTO-BODY SHOP

*Joy holds her drawings up to present them to Trudy, Rudy and Peggy, seated behind Rudy's desk. Christy and Jackie sit behind Joy, observing closely. Joy must speak loudly over the metalworker in the garage.*

> JOY
> *(loud over metal work)*
> The way I looked at it, is this is an opportunity for you to invest in a new business.

*Joy walks backwards to bang on window to get the loudest metal work to stop.*

> Rico!

> PEGGY
> Tell Rico, Dad, number five has got to go off.

*Rudy picks up phone to announce on echoey garage loudspeaker.*

> RUDY
> Rico, number five, no. Off.

*We see Joy through the glass inside the office, from Rico's point of view, pantomiming silently through the glass.*

> JOY
> *(silently pantomimes)*
> Rico, off –

*Rico turns machine off.*

> Thank you!

*Joy unfurls more crayon designs for her idea. Christy watches.*

> It's a standard handle, 53 inches, the sleeve connects to the mop head. Now this is where it gets complicated, there's a clip that connects the sleeve to the, I don't even know what to call it, the cup. Which is connected to the mop head. So when you pull up on the sleeve –

*She uses Christy's crayons as pointer to sketches.*

> – the mop head stretches, so you can wring it without ever touching it with your hands.

*Tony, Rudy, Trudy, Jackie, Peggy, stare.*

TRUDY

The only thing we see is this, um, crayon drawing. We can't make heads or tails.

RUDY

We don't know what it is.

TONY

The mop doesn't hang loose like hair? Like a string?

JOY

It hangs, but not on loose open ends like hair. It's one continuous loop.

TONY

I don't get it.

RUDY

I don't get it, what's he doing here?

TRUDY

What's he doing here?

JOY

He is the father of our children and my friend and he looks out for me.

*Joy stares at them, realizing she must do more to present her idea.*

*Cut to:*


INT. CHRISTY'S ROOM – DAY

*Joy draws further design illustrations, more specific, as Christy and Mimi watch her.*

CHRISTY

We're doing an invention.

*Joy, Mimi and Christy do an imaginary toast with Christy's tea set.*

MIMI

Cheers.

                    JOY
                 (*drawing*)
Yes, we are, Christy.

                  CHRISTY
It's very serious, it's priority.

                    JOY
                 (*drawing*)
Yes it is, Christy.

                  CHRISTY
And I'm helping.

                    JOY
                 (*drawing*)
Yes you are, Christy.

                   TERRY
                (*off-screen*)
Si si, so come in Haiti.

*Joy, Christy, Mimi, look up to see Terry standing in the doorway with Toussaint the plumber.*

Toussaiant is teaching me how to speak French. And the word for industrious is –

                 TOUSSAINT
Taverner.

                   TERRY
Yes. At first I thought something scary might happen, like what happened to Danica when she was kidnapped by that man who turned out to be in hiding from the royal family in Switzerland, and then she moved to Switzerland. Of course she befriended that man, and more. Don't ever try and limit me, Joy. And let me know if you want some of this chakalaka.

                 TOUSSAINT
Chaka, say 'chaka'.

                   TERRY
Chaka.

TOUSSAINT
It's very good.

*Joy, Christy, Mimi stare, taken aback by Terry's blossoming friendship with the plumber.*

INT. RUDY'S TRUCK AUTO-BODY GARAGE – DAY

*Joy, Christy, Jackie walk into Rudy's garage.*

JOY
Hey, Rocky. Hey, Tom.

*A huge piece of truck quarter panel crashes to the floor from a lift. Joy turns to Jackie.*

Take her inside of the office.

*Joy approaches Tino as Jackie and Christy go to the office.*

Hey, Tino.

TINO
Hey.

*Tino, a kind-looking truck metalworker.*

JOY
(*shows crayon drawings*)
I wanted to show you something, will you help me figure this out? I know that has to be welded. This part is supposed to twist.

*She and Tino study the drawings together, while Peggy watches from the side, curious, maybe envious.*

*Cut to:*

*A metal prototype is welded – by Joy – of her mop idea.*

*Prelap dialogue:*

JOY *and* JACKIE
(*off-screen, prelap*)
One, two, three, four, five, six, seven –

*Cut to:*

*Jackie follows, holds her arms out two feet apart as Joy winds soft white cotton yarn around Jackie's extended arms. She counts each loop as she makes it.*

> JOY
>
> . . . Thirty-five, thirty-six, thirty-seven –

> RUDY
>
> What is this?

> JOY
>
> – thirty-eight, thirty-nine, forty. Alright, Dad, come here, grab that right in the middle.

*Rudy gets up, grabs the yarn loops in the middle.*

> Go up.

*Rudy lifts his hand as the ends of the loops on Jackie's arms pull down.*

> Go down.

*Rudy lowers his hand as the ends held by Jackie stretch up.*

> You see it?

> RUDY
>
> Not yet.

*Joy adjusts the cotton loops.*

> JOY
>
> Here, how about now?

> RUDY
>
> No.

> JOY
>
> Well, you're going to.

*Joy takes the forty loops of yarn to the floor where she clips them to the metal mop she welded.*

> RUDY
>
> I don't see it – yet, I mean.

*Joy stands with the metal prototype, the cotton-looped mop head pulled taut –*

JOY

You ready?

*Joy lets go of the sleeve, which slides down, unstretching the mop strands which now hang in a mop of many loops.*

*Everyone looks at this, Joy stares at it.*

Three hundred feet of continuous cotton loop. That's what I drew.

*Joy addresses Trudy, who is behind Rudy's desk with Peggy.*

This, Trudy, is why I am asking for your investment.

*Everyone awaits Trudy's response.*

TRUDY

Morris worked fifty years to earn his fortune, Joy. Before he passed on to the next world, he made me promise on his deathbed that I would never be neglectful with one dollar of the money he so carefully earned. Therefore, you must answer Morris' four questions of financial worthiness. Are you ready?

JOY

I think so. Yes.

TRUDY

Question Number One: where did you go to high school?

JOY

Plainfield Public High.

TRUDY

Question Number Two: who *were* you in high school?

JOY

I was valedictorian.

TRUDY

The smartest student in the school.

RUDY

That's good, right?

TRUDY

Perhaps. Joy might be a brilliant, unrealized creator of commerce. But on the other hand, it's equally possible that she is a fatally flawed underachiever doomed to a lifetime of failure, disappointment and unfulfilled expectations. You must admit, Joy, your life to date makes a stronger case for disappointment.

*Joy looks silently at Trudy, whose words ring true. Suddenly, Peggy seizes the moment.*

PEGGY

I don't care about any of this, it's not only risky but it's fiscally irresponsible and doesn't make any sense whatsoever. Joy's never run a business in her life. I've been running my father's garage for the last ten years.

JOY

Our father.

PEGGY

I have ventures that I'm planning to launch here in this existing business.

JOY

You never mentioned *any* of this till I came to Trudy to ask for an investment today.

JACKIE
(*standing in corner*)

What's Morris' third question?

TRUDY

Are you prepared within six months of commencing this venture to show adequate returns?

*Joy looks at Trudy.*

JOY

I accept your terms.

TONY

Don't do it, Joy.

JACKIE

What's the fourth question?

TRUDY

You are in a room and there is a gun on a table and the only
other person in the room is an adversary in commerce. Only one
of you can prevail, yet you will have protected your business
and Morris' money. Do you pick up the gun, Joy?

JOY

That's a very strange question.

TRUDY

There is nothing strange about this question at all. This. Is.
Money. Do you pick up the gun, Joy, or does the other person?

*Trudy walks closer to Joy, faces her closely.*

Joy, do you pick up the gun?

JOY

I pick up the gun.

TRUDY

Good. I'm going to remember that you said that. When I speak
to my lawyer.

*Joy and Trudy stare each other down.*

CHRISTY
(*prelap, out-of shot*)
What did Trudy's lawyer say?

INT. JOY'S HOUSE, CHRISTY'S BEDROOM – NIGHT

*Joy holds a children's book she has been reading to Christy at
bedtime. Christy is nestled in Joy's arms.*

JOY

He did a worldwide patent search.

CHRISTY

What's a patent?

JOY

A patent is like a law you get to protect your idea. A lot of
people patent their ideas but only a few of them actually get
their ideas made. So, Trudy just wanted to be careful, and this

56

guy found a man that's in Texas, who works for another guy in another country, where they have an idea that *might* be similar to my mop.

CHRISTY

What country?

JOY

Hong Kong.

INT. JOY'S HOUSE, KITCHEN — SAME NIGHT

*As Joy's silhouette approaches the pool of light of the kitchen in the distance, where Rudy and Trudy wait to talk business, Trudy explains her legal advice in prelap.*

TRUDY
(*voice-over*)
The Hong Kong man has a representative in Dallas, Texas. The Dallas man was very reasonable with my lawyer.

*As Joy arrives at the table, Tony and Peggy also sit down with Rudy and Trudy as Tony speaks.*

TONY

So this guy in Texas, we're supposed to pay him a royalty on the patent as protection, right? To be safe from any claims, is that correct?

RUDY

Please, stop using the word 'we', none of this is your money or your business.

TONY

But the same guy also owns a manufacturing plant that you guys say than is cheaper than any other place?

JOY

Yes, in California, a metal and plastic injection-mold factory.

*Tony stares, unsure.*

TONY

Okay. So it's the same guy. He owns the patent and –

TRUDY

This happens all the time in business, you find the best partner,
it's smart –

PEGGY

He doesn't understand business, he doesn't know business.

TONY

I'm always the first to say that but –

PEGGY

I understand business. Dad and I, we buy parts for the trucks all
the time at the garage.

TRUDY

Morris did it all the time, one-stop shopping. It's the cheapest.
That's how he made his money.

TONY

But is it normal that the same guy who has the patent is the
same guy who has the manufacturing plant –

RUDY

Yes.

TRUDY

Yes. Best, better, best. It's better this way.

TONY

And the lawyer, right? Morris' lawyer –

RUDY/TRUDY

Oh yes, he's very good.

TONY

– and he specialized in garment business, not a manufacturing
business.

RUDY

Tony, Tony, Tony, Tony. Let's quit while we're ahead. (*Pause.*)
I know that you want Tony to be your counsellor if you will and
I will respect that as Tony and you should respect what we are
proposing as the lawyer for this whole business endeavor.

*Joy listens as talk swirls on about legalities and complications. On
her face we hear prelap of Clarinda on 'The Private Storm' soap opera:*

58

CLARINDA
(*off-screen, prelap*)
If I don't pursue my dream, I'll be living in hell.

*Cut to:*


INT. TERRY'S BEDROOM – CONTINUOUS

*Terry and Toussaint watch her show on television.*

BARTHOLOMEW
You *are* in hell, but it's a hell I own and operate. Now get back
to work and leave me alone.

*Cut to:*

*Close on Joy, who rips open a box of plastic mop parts.*


INT. RUDY'S SHOP – OFFICE

JOY
The parts have arrived from California and we can start
assembling the mops here. I have the first assembled mop. I told
you it was going to be more refined and it is.

*She proudly holds up her first assembled mop using plastic parts
made by the plant in California. It is light-blue plastic and neatly
designed with taut cotton loops in the 'wringing' position.*

PEGGY
Father Martinez is here with those ladies who keep asking for
jobs.

JOY
Now I finally have jobs for them.

*Joy exits the glass-windowed garage office to the floor of the garage
where Father Martinez, an elderly priest, waits with a group of
twelve new immigrant women who want work. Music begins.*

JOY
(*in Spanish*)
Hola, gracias por venir, padre.

PRIEST

Hola, Joy, me trajo un monton de la iglesia para que en busca de trabajo.

JOY

Hola, como estas.

EUCARIA

Este es mi primo's y nino's.

*Joy shakes their hands.*

JOY

Este trabajo consistira en la costura de la cabeza del algodon.

*She picks up a looped mop head to show how it needs to be sewn together.*

INT. HANGAR SPACE OF ADJOINING BUILDING – DAY

*Where Joy and Jackie show Eucaria and the women clean neat work tables, the parts, and how to assemble them and sew what needs to be sewn. Five simple spinning looms make the forty loops per mop.*

*Rudy, Trudy, Peggy watch.*

RUDY

I'm a little proud of you, I got to admit it.

*Cut to:*

INT. RUDY'S GARAGE – CONTINUOUS

TRUDY

*But*, it cost much more than fifteen thousand to make the first run.

JOY

I know, Trudy, but in fairness, that wasn't my fault –

RUDY

There's a fax coming in with another bill right now from California.

*Rudy rips paper from fax machine, holds it up.*

This guy keeps billing me for his mistakes.

TRUDY

That's business.

JOY

It's not how I do business.

*She dials the phone, calls the California manufacturer.*

JOY
(*on phone*)

Gerhart, I'm not gonna keep paying for these parts it's taking you four times to get right.

GERHART
(*off-screen, on phone*)

That was your design, that's mold-making, that's the process. My clients pay when we figure it out.

JOY

It was not my design, Gerhart, it was your mistake. I'm not paying it.

GERHART

That was your design, you have to pay –

*Joy hangs up.*

TRUDY

Did you just hang up on him?

JOY

This guy was supposed to be easy and inexpensive. He keeps over-billing us, I'm not paying for it.

*Joy points firmly to everyone in the room.*

*Nobody* pay it. I'm going to fight it out with this guy.

TRUDY

Just assemble them and try to sell them.

PEGGY

See if you can sell them before Trudy spends any more money.

EXT. FRONT OF CHARLIE'S HARDWARE – DAY

*Joy stands with store owner – Charlie, sixty-five.*

> JOY
> Just put it in your window, Charlie, let your costumers decide.
> My family's been going to you my whole life.

> CHARLIE
> The big companies pay me for my shelf space, that's how I stay
> in business. Maybe you can get one of those companies to sell
> your mop, Joy.

EXT. PRE-WAR OFFICE BUILDING, AMERICAN FLAG ON TOP –
DAY

*Joy marches to the corporate building with determination, sample
mop, purse and a binder of sales ideas in her hands.*

> JOY
> (off-screen, prelap)
> It's expensive at 19.95, but it's the only mop you'll ever have to
> buy, with the most absorbent cotton on the first self-wringing
> mop.

INT. MOP COMPANY VICE PRESIDENT'S OFFICE – DAY

*Joy sits in her wool winter coat as Harold, the veteran Vice President
of the large housewares corporation, talks from behind his big wood
desk in his wood-paneled office.*

> MOP EXECUTIVE
> But I don't want people to buy one mop for twenty dollars and
> never have to buy another mop again. I'd rather they keep
> buying our mops at five dollars, fifty times, a hundred times.

*Joy listens, doesn't understand.*

> Look, you were broke, bored, you had an idea, so what, lots of
> people have ideas. Please, go home, lady, take care of your
> family.

*Joy stares at him.*

EXT. K-MART PARKING LOT – OVERCAST DAY

*Wide shot of slushy snowy parking lot. As customers pass her by, Joy tries to get their attention to demonstrate the mop with her three-by-four linoleum pad on the asphalt. Christy stands to the side mopping on a square of cardboard.*

> JOY

Would you like to try a new mop? It's the only mop you will ever have to buy.

*Women shoppers pass her by, ignoring her.*

Hi, would you like to try the new mop? It's self-wringing, you can remove the mop head, throw it in the wash, no germs. Look, it's – Hi, you wanna try it? You can just – It self-wrings, see. No other mop does this.

*Joy stops, frustrated, lets the mop fall from her hand to the ground, points to someone off-screen. Christy takes her mother's hand and they walk out of the wide frame of the parking lot, leaving behind their linoleum and mops.*

*Jackie walks into the frame, picks up the mop and begins to pitch.*

> JACKIE
> (*mopping*)

Come try the brand new mop, it's the mop of the future.

*Joy and Christy walk into frame pretending to be customers, past Jackie on their way to the K-Mart.*

You want to try this mop, ladies?

> JOY

What's this?

> JACKIE

A brand new mop. You can wring it without getting your hands dirty.

> JOY

Nah, I don't think so.

*She walks away.*

JACKIE

Come on, try it. It's the mop of the future.

*Joy stops, turns around.*

JOY

Self-wringing, huh?

JACKIE

Yeah.

JOY

I do like the idea of that, ya know, I hate having to touch the mop head after I get done cleaning the bathroom floor. I always think that's disgusting.

*A few women customers pause to watch Joy try the mop.*

It really does get all the corners the sponge mop won't get. All those crannies where my kids spill juice.

CHRISTY

I really like it, can we buy it?

JOY

Take it easy, Christy. You know what would make it really great would be if you could take the mop head and put it in the wash.

JACKIE

You can.

JOY

What? Are you serious?

JACKIE

Yes.

JOY

How much is this mop?

JACKIE

$19.95.

JOY

But if it's the only mop you ever buy –

JACKIE

It is.

Hi, Daddy.

*Joy looks up to see Tony, Angela Starpoli, and Angela's two brothers, walking up on their way out of K-Mart with bags. Tony stares at Joy and Christy.*

TONY
You remember Angela and her two brothers, right?

JOY
Yes, I do. Hi, how are you?

*Angela stares as if Joy is pathetic for what she is doing.*

CHRISTY
Mommy, the policeman.

*Joy turns around to see cops approach. She hastily starts to pack up her merchandise, but the cops take it.*

COP I
Ma'am, I'm taking this merchandise. You cannot sell on K-Mart property.

JOY
No, sir, we were just leaving. We were leaving, sir.

COP I
Now I'm going to give you a warning. If I catch you out here again you *will* be prosecuted. You cannot sell on K-Mart property.

JOY
I just feel if the customers could see the mop, please. I made those myself, I paid for them. Please. I won't come back but you don't have to take my stuff.

COP I
You cannot sell on K-Mart property.

*The cops leave with all her merchandise. Joy, Jackie and Christy are left standing, staring at Tony, Angela and her brothers. Christy struggles to hold back tears.*

ANGELA
How embarrassing for you, to be seen here like this with your daughter. What kind of parent are you?

BROTHER 1

What a great mother you are.

JOY
(*humiliated*)

Hey, guys we don't need to –

*Christy starts crying. Joy goes to her, kneels, holds her.*

BROTHER 2

What are you doing? In this weather, have your kid out here with no gloves.

JOY

Hey.

*She stands and takes Christy back to the car.*

TONY

Enough, enough, stop it.

BROTHER

Let's go.

ANGELA

Tony, let's go.

TONY

I'm coming, I'm coming.

*He keeps watching Joy and Christy at the car as Joy kicks to open her dented door with the creak. She finally gets in. Jackie sits next to Joy, Christy in back seat. They sit in silence. Christy is still kind of crying. Joy lowers her head to the steering wheel, feeling very alone.*

EXT. DRIVEWAY OF JOY'S HOUSE – NIGHT

*Joy kicks the gate to her yard open, arms full of binders, notebooks, a coffee mug, keys, purse, papers, Christy walks with her. On the porch, she kicks broken wood pillar back into it's spot.*

JOY
(*pissed*)

Stupid thing, this place is following apart.

*Certified letter from the telephone company, taped to the front door.*

NO, noooooo.

66

*Joy tears the certified letter from the door, goes inside.*

INT. JOY'S HOUSE – CONTINUOUS

> MIMI
> Honey, the telephone isn't working.

> JOY
> I know, I just got the notice.

> MIMI
> I had to go next door to use the phone. Tommy's got a fever.

> JOY
> Tommy has a fever?

> MIMI
> Simple cold with a cough, it's going around, all the kids have it.
> Thank God the heat's still working.

> CHRISTY
> (*holds phone*)
> Mommy, why isn't the phone working?

*Christy coughs.*

> JOY
> Because I'm late paying the bill.

> CHRISTY
> Are we going to lose our house?

> JOY
> No, we're not going to lose our house.

*Christy coughs.*

> Not you too, Christy.

*She feels Christy's forehead.*

> Come on, get upstairs, get in the bath.

*Joy walks Christy up the stairs as Mimi shouts from downstairs.*

> MIMI
> Listen to your mommy, get right in that tub.

CHRISTY

I don't want a hot bath.

JOY

I don't care.

*Joy picks up Christy as she walks upstairs.*

MIMI

Christy, you get in that hot bath, listen to your mother, I don't want you getting sick too.

*Upstairs, Joy runs the bath.*

CHRISTY

Lauren Wells said you were a cleaning lady and sell used mops.

JOY

Lauren Wells said that?

*She pulls Christy's sweater over her head.*

CHRISTY

Yeah, and it really hurt my feelings.

*Joy brushes Christy's hair to the side.*

JOY

First of all, even if I was a cleaning lady, so what, there's no shame in hard work. And second of all I'm trying to sell a new mop, not used mops. And third of all don't, don't take any guff from anybody. You know, don't let it in. I know it's hard.

*Christy and she share a stare together.*

I'm sorry that happened. Now get in the bath.

*Christy nods. Joy closes the door behind her, enters Tommy's room.*

INT. TOMMY'S ROOM – CONTINUOUS

*Joy sits on the bed, watches Tommy sleeping. Leans down, kisses him. Sits alone on the bed in a moment of solitude bordering on despair. Tommy coughs.*

JOY
(whispers)

Honey, please go to sleep.

*Joy walks downstairs in a cloud of emotion, passes Mimi folding laundry.*

> MIMI

Joy.

> JOY

What now, Mimi?

> MIMI

Joy, wait, wait, tell me what happened today, I want to know how it went. Please, I want to know.

*Joy stops turns and faces Mimi.*

> JOY
> (*whisper*)

It was a disaster.

> MIMI
> (*quietly*)

But you must never give up. Ever since you were little, you were born to bear –

> JOY

Bear what, Mimi? Failure, disgrace, humiliation in front of my daughter?

> MIMI

You were born to be the unanxious presence in the room. And I know that I'm going to live to see you grow to be the successful matriarch you were born to be.

> JOY

Matriarch, ha.

*Doorbell rings.*

> MIMI

To be a mother with courage.

> JOY

Who can't even support her children.

*Joy walks toward door.*

Sweetheart.

*Joy opens front door to see Tony.*

JOY

What are you doing here?

INT. JOY'S LIVING ROOM

TONY

I have this idea, a guy I know.

JOY

What guy?

TONY

He used to work with me at Campbell's, and now he works at this big retailer, a new way of doing business. It's worth a try.

JOY

You would do that for me?

TONY

Of course.

GRANDMA MIMI
(*voice-over*)

They were the best divorced couple in America, much better friends than when they were husband and wife, and it only got better with time.

TONY

I can get you a meeting with him.

JOY

Where is it?

*Prelap: clopping of horses on pavement.*

EXT. LANCASTER PENNSYLVANIA/INT. JOY'S CAR – DAY

*Tony drives Joy's car. Ahead of them an Amish horse and wagon clops along the road. To the sides, farmland.*

                          JOY

I don't understand what we're doing in Amish country, they
don't even have electricity out here, how could they sell
anything on TV?

                          TONY

It has nothing to do with Aimish people it just happens to be
located here. I looked it up, in Aimish country.

*Smirk on Joy's face because of the way Tony pronounces Amish.*

                          JOY
                      (*correctly*)

Ah-mish.

                          TONY

What?

                          JOY

Ah-mish.

                          TONY

Aim-ish.

*Wide shot: a large single modern corporate four-storey building
straight ahead in the middle of farmland. Joy's car approaches.*


INT. QVC HEADQUARTERS AND TV STUDIO, LANCASTER, PA

*Joy and Tony walk into a huge lobby with a high ceiling. Far away is
the reception desk. Joy carries mops, bucket, foldable section of
white linoleum floor.*

                      RECEPTIONIST

Sign in, please.

                          TONY

We are here to see Marv Brickman.

                      RECEPTIONIST

Okay, Marv Brickman, does he know who you are if I call his
office?

                          TONY

Of course, he knows we were friends, we used to work together.

*Joy and Tony sit. And wait. On a bench sofa that goes the entire length of the lobby.*

*In a wide shot: Joy and Tony look very small sitting there. Different angles of them sitting, waiting, time passing.*

*Closer on Joy and Tony. They hear a door open, they turn to hear three businessmen in suits, forties, laughing, talking, approaching.*

*Joy and Tony sit up, hopeful. But the businessmen walk past. Joy and Tony sit back, continue to wait.*

*Till eventually door opens, and a businessman walks into frame, seen only from the waist down as Tony stands to greet him but camera remains low, seated with Joy, looking up at the two men in the foreground, whose faces and shoulders are above the frame. Joy sits framed between them.*

> MARV BRICKMAN
> (*deep voice whispers*)

Tonyyyyy.

> TONY

Marv, how are you?

> MARV BRICKMAN

I can't see you today.

> TONY

Why?

> MARV BRICKMAN
> (*whisper*)

Maybe tomorrow if you can stay in town.

*Camera remains on Joy looking up at the standing men, talking, half out of frame.*

> TONY
> (*off-screen, hushed*)

No, we left the kids at home, we can't. We can't stay until tomorrow.

> MARV BRICKMAN

Listen, you can't just expect to come in here and see someone.

*Another man enters the frame, also only half seen, like Tony and Marv, crosses frame, almost leaves it. He is tall in plaidish*

*Midwestern suit pants, Tattersall shirt-sleeves, tie, big-ten university football ring on big right hand, wedding band on his left, with briefcase and suit coat: Neil Walker.*

*Joy is visible only through the slight space now between the tall standing men, looking up at them (their top halves above frame).*

> NEIL WALKER
> (*off-screen*)
> Did you take care of that advertising thing?

> MARV BRICKMAN
>
> Yes.

*Camera racks focus to Neil's hand by his side, with Michigan State University ring.*

> NEIL WALKER
> Good. Who are you talking to here?

> MARV BRICKMAN
> (*off-screen*)
> This is my good friend Tony –

> TONY
>
> Tony Miranda.

*Joy watches the men shake hands above her head.*

> MARV BRICKMAN
> (*off-screen*)
> We worked together at Campbell's. This is his ex-wife –

*Neil's hand reaches out to shake Joy's as she remains seated.*

> NEIL WALKER
> (*off-screen*)
>
> Neil Walker.

> JOY
>
> Joy.

*They shake hands.*

> MARV BRICKMAN
> She's an inventor, she wanted two minutes of your time today,
> but Neil, don't worry about this, maybe tomorrow –

73

> NEIL WALKER
> (*off-screen*)
> You know what, why don't you come in for five minutes while the sales group is still here.

*Joy's face lights up.*

> JOY

OK.

> MARV BRICKMAN

Neil, are you sure?

> NEIL WALKER

Yeah, absolutely.

> TONY

Thank you.

> NEIL WALKER

Yeah, you got everything?

> JOY

Yeah.

> NEIL WALKER

Great.

*Tony and Marv hug in foreground as Joy walks far away into the building with Neil.*

> TONY
> (*turns and hugs Marv*)
> Thank you, man.

*Joy looks back at Tony as he grows small behind her, watching her disappear into this new world around a corner with Neil.*

INT. NEIL WALKER'S OFFICE – CONTINUOUS

*Camera begins on Neil's hand on the table, with the ring, and goes up his brown houndstooth sports jacket, to find the ruddy face of this sincere, four-square, no-nonsense, with deep Mid-West sales experience, man – in close up – looking to the far side of the conference room.*

74

NEIL WALKER
(*deep voice*)
So, tell us your name please.

JOY
(*standing*)
I'm Joy.

*Joy stands awkwardly, nervously, in her wool coat, holding her mop handle, facing the glass conference table of five male sales execs, thirty to forty-five, and one older woman secretary, and Neil at the head of the table.*

NEIL WALKER
And what did you like to show us today?

JOY
I have a self-wringing mop.

*Camera remains on Neil's close up as we hear Joy dip the mop in water to begin her demonstration across room.*

NEIL WALKER
Do you need some help?

JOY
No, no, I – uh –

*We hear Joy accidentally slosh the bucket of water on the shoe of a Sales Rep, fifty.*

SALES REP
(*off-screen*)
That's my shoe –

*Laughter at the conference table.*

JOY
(*off-screen*)
Oh my goodness, I'm so sorry, sir.

*More laughter at the conference table.*

Now your shoe is very clean.

*Cut to:*

*Joy on her knees, wiping the man's shoe with a paper napkins close to the bucket.*

75

*Neil watches from the far end of the table.*

> NEIL WALKER
> Is that plastic?

> JOY
> Yes.

*Close on Neil all through:*

> NEIL WALKER
> Arnold, why don't you give it a try it, is that okay –

> JOY
> (*off-screen*)
> Yes, of course.

*Off-screen, Arnold, fifty-five, little bit of a pot belly, tie, takes the mop as Joy unfolds the linoleum square she has brought. Guys laugh as he uses the mop and looks at them like 'What the hell am I doing?'*

> Just dunk it.

> ARNOLD
> (*off-screen*)
> I dip it.

> JOY
> (*off-screen*)
> Yes.

> ARNOLD
> (*off-screen*)
> And then I ah, twist it.

> JOY
> (*off-screen*)
> Well, then you have to pull first, pull it and twist it.

> SALES REP
> (*laughing, off-screen*)
> You have to pull it first and then you twist it.

> ARNOLD
> (*off-screen*)
> I am pulling it and I am twisting it.

76

*Men laugh off-screen.*

SALES EXECS

A little harder. Just like when you're on the road.

*Cut to:*

*Joy looks humiliated as they all laugh.*

NEIL WALKER

We don't mean to be disrespectful, Joy, it's the end of a long day for us.

*All laughter stops. Quiet. Neil takes control. Slowly. Steadily. Confidently. No nonsense.*

I feel like I want to tell you a little bit about who I am, because I have a feeling you don't know exactly where you are right now, am I right?

*Joy gives a small humble nod.*

Ten months ago, a man named Barry Diller called me from Los Angeles. He started a television network, Fox television channel. Prior to that he ran Twentieth Century Fox, among other studios, and he acquired a little cable channel right here in Lancaster, Pennsylvania, and he hired me to run it, as a bigger idea. Now, I'm from Detroit, Michigan. I ran America's largest, most affordable, successful, value-driven retailer: a chain called K-Mart. Prior to that I was a buyer for K-Mart, and prior to that I managed seven separate K-Mart stores. I decide what products we let into our stores here, into people's homes, twenty-four hours a day, for our valued customers. I choose very carefully and very conservatively. I spend most of my day deflecting incoming shots from people like yourself. (*Serious as a heart attack.*) Do you see that chart?

*He rises from his chair and walks over to the chart by Joy.*

This green line here either rises or stays the same each month. There's no problem with my product choice.

*He turns and walks up to Joy, face to face.*

Do you know what QVC stands for, Joy?

No, I don't.

NEIL WALKER

Quality, value, convenience. I sell product affordably, but I don't sell cheap product. Your mop is plastic and it looks strange.

*Joy stares at Neil.*

JOY

I don't know anything about – charts or – business, frankly, but I do clean my own home and I made this mop because it is better than anything else out there. Please give me a chance.

INT. BIG EMPTY WHITE FORMICA PRODUCT-TESTING KITCHEN AND BATHROOM SET – DAY

*Joy mops the Formica floor near the open white bathroom.*

JOY
(*mopping*)

I like that it's plastic, because it's so light in my hands, it's like nothing. It's also ten times more absorbent than any other mop on the market. Why, because of three hundred feet of continuous cotton loop, that I looped myself, that's an enormous amount of absorbent cotton on a very small mop head. Now I'm done with the bathroom and I haven't wrung the mop once. Let me ask you a question, would you take this mop where you were just cleaning the bathroom and around the toilet and all of those germs and take it into the kitchen? (*She walks over to the kitchen area.*) Where your family eats and you feed your children? I take this mop head, I put it in the washing machine, it comes out clean like new. You can't do that with *any* other mop. So –

NEIL WALKER

Stop.

*He stares at her.*

Can you make fifty thousand mops by next week?

*Joy pauses in shock before she speaks quietly.*

Yeah. I think so.

INT. QVC HALLWAY – CONTINUOUS

*Neil leads Joy into a big backstage room, buzzing with costume racks, props, make-up chairs, people, changing rooms, like at a film studio.*

NEIL WALKER

David Selznick, the son of immigrants, married Jennifer Jones, from Oklahoma, America's sweetheart. That just goes to show you that in America, the ordinary meets the extraordinary every single day. Anything is possible. No matter who you are.

*Neil stops costumers Roger and Thomas as they roll a rack of pants twenty feet to the side.*

Thomas, where are you going with that?

COSTUMER THOMAS

These the skinny pants you wanted.

NEIL WALKER

No, I never said skinny pants, I said stove pipe. The classic look.

COSTUMER THOMAS

I heard skinny pants.

COSTUMER ROGER

Yeah. I heard skinny pants.

NEIL WALKER

No, you know how much I love the stove pipe. Classic look.

COSTUMER THOMAS

Stove pipe, classic.

COSTUMER ROGER

Got it, Got it, Got it.

COSTUMER THOMAS

Fine we'll go with stove pipe.

*Neil resumes his walk with Joy through the large backstage area.*

NEIL WALKER
(*walking*)

See, those guys, I told them so many times and they still don't understand. A very smart guy once said, 'You tell somebody something once, they don't listen. You tell somebody four times, they don't listen. By the ninth time you say it, they *begin* to hear you.' That's why I have to tell them about the stove pipes, that's why we're on twenty-four hours a day. (*Turns to face bald spokesmodel who walks up.*) What's up, Todd?

TODD MALE SPOKESMODEL
Music in the make-up rooms?

NEIL WALKER
Yes, I thought it gave a sense of place, but you have every option, you can turn it down, Todd. You're our number-one seller.

CINDY SPOKESMODEL
What? *He's* your seller?

*She stands from a make-up table and storms off.*

NEIL WALKER
Cindy, no, please, you know that we love you.

*Cindy slams a dressing-room door.*

Oh for heaven's sake.

TODD MALE SPOKESMODEL
She's never had a professional attitude, clearly she's jealous.

NEIL WALKER
Could you do me a favor, Todd, and make her your friend? Could you just do me that favor, Todd? Please, for me?

TODD MALE SPOKESMODEL
Yes, sir.

NEIL WALKER
Thank you. Now this is Joy, she has a very exciting new mop we're going to introduce next week, I'd like you to launch it, you're my first choice.

A mop, you want me to bring this newborn into the world?

JOY

Well, that newborn you're holding has every cent, every dollar, even debt, I've ever made.

TODD MALE SPOKESMODEL

Every cent you've ever made?

JOY

That's right.

TODD MALE SPOKESMODEL

That kind of pressure's not helpful.

JOY

What?

TODD MALE SPOKESMODEL

It's not part of my process, either.

JOY

Oh.

*Todd walks off to his dressing room.*

NEIL WALKER

Todd.

JOY

I didn't mean to pressure you.

NEIL WALKER

Performers can be finicky creatures. But trust me he is our number-one seller. He is selling everything through the roof at numbers we never seen before. I take it very seriously I see it as a privilege that we have to go into people's homes and I despise anyone who's cynical about that. Jack Warner wasn't cynical about that, Darryl Zanuck wasn't cynical about that and Neil Walker is not cynical about that. Let me show you the stage.

*Joy follows him down a very dark backlit corridor – backstage somewhere – dark.*

*They walk along the back of sets, along a curved wall.*

NEIL WALKER

I believe eventually, one day, television will even be by and
about everyday regular people. Maybe even on computers.
Who knows, no one thought this network would be real, and
here we are. By the way, the stock's going through the roof –

*Joy jumps back, as the curved wall suddenly starts to move and
rotate with a sliding sound of rotating architecture.*

*A dog barks.*

We must be mindful of Joan's dog.

*Joy is enchanted to scoop up a little dog next to the rotating stage.*

JOY

Who's Joan?

*Suddenly Joan Rivers takes the dog from Joy's arms as she stands on
a brilliantly colored set that rotates past them.*

JOAN RIVERS

Thank you, darling. Oh Mr. Peepers, you were almost a Peepers
pancake. You gotta be careful, boy.

*Joy is amazed as she watches Joan rotate away from her. Neil
resumes walking with her.*

NEIL WALKER

It's a round stage that has four or five different sets that rotate,
depending on what we're selling at a given moment.

*They turn a corner to see where the cameras are, the wires, the
microphones, a series of tables with forty people answering phones
for orders. A brightly closured set rotates into place and stops – with
Joan and Cindy seated in beautiful chairs.*

Here comes Joan and Cindy. Watch this, these guys are major.
Joan's the original seller.

JOAN RIVERS
(*off-screen*)
You're just starting your jewelry wardrobe. Can you do

anything better than this – you're going to mix in your blacks, your golds, your pearls.

CINDY *and* JOAN RIVERS
Everything.

CINDY
Look at it against the peach.

JOAN RIVERS
Okay.

CINDY
Morning. Look at this.

JOAN RIVERS
Green.

CINDY
Afternoon.

JOAN RIVERS
Look.

CINDY
Black, evening.

JOAN RIVERS
Of course the night.

CINDY
I mean, can you be more elegant? So it's functional, elegant –

JOAN RIVERS
You can wear it alone.

*Cut to:*

*Neil and Joy on set still looking on.*

NEIL WALKER
(*quietly*)
Stars and people, they always make the mistake and think it's about the face. But it's not, it's about the hands. Because that's what people use, they hold things they care about. And her hands are going to become their hands, and that becomes them. And then their voice and their eyes. Stars always make the

83

mistake, it's really about the hands and the voice. That's the heart of it.

CINDY

Just $39, number J6276. Hundred-dollar value, are they not phenomenal?

NEIL WALKER

Now, watch this. Cindy is going to lay this down right –

*He holds his hand up in suspense.*

CINDY

But you need to call in right now, $39.99.

NEIL WALKER

*Now.* (*Points at Cindy.*)

CINDY

(*points at camera*)
You need this, you can get this, you need to call right now, though. I am being told we have limited inventory left.

*Phones begin ringing off the hook. Neil walks Joy past the rows of people answering phones at the back of the sound stage.*

NEIL WALKER

Watch the calls come in, watch the calls. Here they come, here they come. Now, calls, calls, calls, calls, calls, calls, look at the count.

*He points to an illuminated board of rolling numbers, counting the orders, on the wall.*

Counting, you see it starts at 18,000. I guarantee you it will go over 20,000. Those are real numbers those are FTC standards. Those are legal, those are actual sales, Joy. The lines are busy? Are the cues full?

STAGE MANAGER

Yes, they're all full.

NEIL WALKER

Okay, we need a phone call right now. Keep this going. Phone call right now. When people can't get through to order, we have to take a call to keep them watching till they can dial through.

CINDY
(*off-screen*)
We have a caller, we have a caller, ah, Sharon from Colorado.
Hey, Sharon.

JOAN RIVERS
Hey, Sharon.

CALLER SHARON
(*on speaker*)
Cindy and Joan I can't believe I'm talking to you.

*Neil Walker paces before the phone bank.*

NEIL WALKER
YES. YES. YES. YES. YES.

CINDY
Are you happy with your necklaces?

CALLER SHARON
These necklaces are so gorgeous and timeless.

CINDY
Do you like it?

CALLER SHARON
I'm so excited to have these.

*Neil motioning to the stage.*

NEIL WALKER
Keep it going, keep it going. Keep it going. Yes. Yes. Yes. Watch
the counter, Joy.

*Joy walks towards him.*

See the counter, see those numbers. Were going to wind up at
25,000. Cindy knows how to close it.

JOY
Wow.

NEIL WALKER
Okay, I want you to go home, I want you to talk to your lawyer,
look at your contract, make sure your product factory is in line.

*Joy nods.*

Okay?

JOY

Okay.

NEIL WALKER

Okay. Godspeed, good luck, here we go. I'll walk you out.

EXT. RUDY'S GARAGE, GUN RANGE

*Men shooting.*

INT. RUDY'S OFFICE – DAY

RUDY

You can't expect Trudy to write a check for $200,000 for 50,000 mops when you already owe her $18,000 to make mops you haven't even sold yet.

*Joy stares at Rudy, Trudy, Peggy, who stare coldly.*

JOY

Do you understand that there is a business that wants to sell my mop on television. It's going to sell.

RUDY

Fine, you feel so strongly about it, you put up half the money.

TRUDY

Yes, it's only fair that you share the financial risk, too.

PEGGY

How's she going to do that? She's got nothing. She's got no money.

JOY

What, do you want me to take out a second mortgage on my house?

*Rudy and Trudy and Peggy stare at Joy.*

*Joy walks out of Rudy's office, past a very concerned Tony and Jackie.*

JOY
(*walking*)

They want me to take out a second mortgage on my house.

TONY
(*walking*)

A second mortgage?

JACKIE
(*walking*)

But the house, the kids, Joy.

TONY

What's going to happen, Joy? How will you do that?

JOY

I don't know.

*Joy goes out the garage door and for the first time walks through the old wood fence over to the junk yard gun range. She approaches Earl, who stands alone with a shotgun.*

JOY

Hey, how you doing?

EARL

Hey, you know I've been watching you through that fence since you were a little girl? I've been watching you grow up.

JOY
(*looks at his shotgun*)

Hey, listen. You think it would be okay if I –

EARL

You want to fire a few rounds?

JOY

I do.

EARL

Yeah, it might make you feel better.

JOY

Thank you. I think it will.

EARL
*(handing her the shotgun)*
You know how to hold it?

JOY
I think so, yeah.

*Joy aims the shotgun, pumps and fires the rifle. Four times.*

GUN RANGE OWNER
Yeah. Good. Good. Good.

*Joy lowers the gun. She exhales lots of tension for a moment, just standing there.*

*Cut to:*


INT. JOY'S LIVING ROOM – NIGHT

*Joy turns on the TV, sits surrounded by Mimi, Jackie, Christy, Tony, Rudy, Trudy, Peggy at the back. Terry sits alone on a chair to the side, excited. We hear Todd, the spokesmodel on TV, off-screen.*

TODD MALE SPOKESMODEL
*(off-screen)*
Get ready, this is definitely gonna change the holiday for anyone who has a floor or a bathroom, because we have the most exciting new home product in years. This is the new self-wringing mop. This is the new standard in homes, right here. Let's take a look at this. This is brought to you only by QVC.

*Joy, Tony, Rudy, Terry, Trudy, Jackie, all watch tense, excited.*

Now this is clearly extremely soft and absorbent cotton. Here we go. You just take this. And you, uh, and you start – I'm not sure. This is a little trickier than it looks –

*Everyone is tense, with Joy's face at the centre.*

TODD MALE SPOKESMODEL
*(off-screen)*
Whoops it's getting my arm wet there. Ah, let's see. We've got no sales here.

*Push in on Joy's face quietly dying.*

TODD MALE SPOKESMODEL
(*off-screen*)
Maybe a call. Is there a call? So there are no calls. Alright. And
we do not have any sales still so here's what we're going to do.
We're going to move on now. We're going to move on to Cindy
who's going to talk to Serena Kendall, former star from *Falcon
Crest* and *Dynasty*, and she's going to tell us all about her new
line of gowns.

*On TV, we see Cindy with Serena Kendall, and a Model wearing a
gown.*

SERENA KENDALL
These are my special occasion gowns –

CINDY
Special. How apropos –

SERENA KENDALL
– that were inspired by all of the times that I was in *Dynasty*
and *Falcon Crest*.

CINDY
That is absolutely amazing. I want you to pan in. Look at these.

SERENA KENDALL
Look at the detail.

CINDY
Look at the detail.

SERENA KENDALL
Look at the value in that.

CINDY
About how many sequins would you say that is?

*Push in on Terry, crushed by the fail.*

RUDY
That's it?

TRUDY
That's all?

PEGGY
Yeah, it's over, that's how fast it happens on TV.

MIMI

No, they're going to give her a second chance.

PEGGY

No, they're not gonna give her a second chance. That's not what's gonna happen. In business you strike out and you're out.

MIMI

They're going to give her a second chance. They will.

TRUDY

200,000 dollars.

RUDY

50,0000 mops.

*Joy walks to turn off the TV, ignoring Tony trying to stop to comfort her. She stands in devastated silence as everyone sits watching her. A very tense pause.*

*The phone suddenly rings. Joy turns, walks toward the phone. Terry puts her hand out to Joy's shoulder –*

TERRY

Joy –

*Joy ignores Terry, in crushed shock, answers the phone.*

*Cut to:*


INT. QVC STAGE

*Cindy and Serena Kendall sell the gown.*

CINDY

How many sequins would you say that is?

SERENA KENDALL

2,107.

CINDY

For, get this, how much?

SERENA KENDALL

$299.

CINDY
(*gasps*)

GAHHHHH.

*Cut to:*

*Neil's hand signing a paper on a clipboard, speaking into phone.*

JOY
(*softly*)

Hello.

NEIL WALKER
(*on phone*)

I'm sorry the product didn't sell.

JOY

That man didn't know what he was doing, Neil.

NEIL WALKER
(*on phone*)

Well, it wasn't the man, Joy. It was the product.

JOY

I made 50,000 units because you told me to, I mortgaged my house, I'm in 200,000 dollars of debt. More.

NEIL WALKER
(*on phone*)

Well, it's your business, it's your debt and we indemnify up to a third if you read the contract. To be honest that's even going to be hard to get.

JOY

Neil, you've got to give us another chance.

NEIL WALKER

I'm so sorry, Joy. I just can't bring it to my boss. I can't.

JOY
(*whispers*)

Well, I can't accept your answer. I can't and I won't.

*She hangs up. We stay on Joy's face as she slowly walks from the phone with angry determination in her eyes..*

RUDY
(*off-screen*)
Joy, you have to let Trudy report this loss in bankruptcy because
otherwise she's going to hemorrhage even more money. *You*
have to file too, because you –

EXT. AMISH COUNTRY, LANCASTER, PA – DAY

*Joy's old car drives through the roads.*

RUDY
(*voice-over*)
– you mortgaged your children's future and you lost, and you
have to prepare yourself for that.

TRUDY
(*voice-over*)
You have to file for bankruptcy.

PEGGY
(*voice-over*)
I warned you so many times, Joy. Dad, I warned you not to
spend her money.

INT. UPSTAIRS OFFICES OF QVC – CONTINUOUS

*We track behind Joy in her wool coat with her hair in a braided
ponytail as she storms down the corporate corridor. Neil spots Joy in
shock, sitting in a glass walled conference room.*

*In a meeting in the glass conference room, Neil looks over his
shoulder and turns in part shock that Joy is storming in.*

*Joy bursts into the glass conference room mid-meeting and sits down
opposite Neil.*

NEIL WALKER
I'm in a meeting with our lawyers, what do you think you're
doing?

*Joy ignores the others in the room and speaks only to Neil as if they
are the only two there.*

'Go home, Joy, and watch the numbers roll in on television.'
Make 50,000 mops, borrowing and owing every dollar
including your home.

NEIL WALKER

It could have been handled better. I'll let Todd have another
shot.

JOY

I don't want Todd or anyone else to try it. It should be me.

NEIL WALKER

We don't have regular people. We have celebrities or
spokesmodels do the selling. I told you this.

JOY

Who sold you the mop, who sold it to *you*? Who taught *you*
how to use it and who convinced you that it was great after you
thought it was worthless?

*Neil looks at the rest of the room.*

NEIL WALKER

Excuse me, can you give us a second?

*He gets up.*

Come with me.

*He leads Joy out of the room.*


INT. HALLWAY OUTSIDE OF CONFERENCE ROOM

*Neil turns and immediately counters Joy's argument.*

NEIL WALKER

Have you ever been in front of a TV camera? You comfortable
in front of a TV camera? Because when you get there, there's
lights and there's cameras and people freeze up.

JOY

You said to me that David Selznick, the son of immigrants
married Jennifer Jones, an all-American girl from Oklahoma,
because in America, all races and all classes can meet and make

whatever opportunities they can and that is what you feel when you reach into people's homes with what you sell. You said that.

*Neil stares at Joy for three seconds.*

INT. QVC – BACKSTAGE

*Cut to:*

*Joy's hair elegantly done in the back. Neil watching.*

> NEIL WALKER
> Yeah, yeah, yeah, beautiful. Very bold. Very classic. Alright, if you come back next time – (*To Hairdresser Lori.*) Lori, Lori, I want you to just put the hair a little bit forward like that if she comes back again. Okay? Not with the comb, not with the comb.

*Thomas holds up a white dress and a black dress.*

> Try the black, okay? It's going to be perfect.

> JOY
> Alright.

*Joy takes the dress into dressing room, and looks back as the door closes.*

*Neil waits for her to step out – finally – beautiful in the fitted black dress and heels.*

> NEIL WALKER
> Wow. Beautiful, what do you think, how do you feel?

*Joy stands looking uncomfortable.*

> JOY
> I'd like to change just one thing, would you mind?

> NEIL WALKER
> Okay, surprise me.

> JOY
> One small thing. I'll surprise you.

> NEIL WALKER
> Okay, surprise me.

*Joy closes door and Neil waits patiently.*

What would be the small thing that she changes?

*Joy opens the door again, looks at Neil unblinking with her hair half down, now dressed in a white blouse and pants*

*What?* You undid the whole thing.

JOY

This is me.

NEIL WALKER

This is you? You've got on the exact same outfit you had when you came in here.

JOY

I wear a blouse and I wear pants. That's who I am. I'm want to go on as me.

NEIL WALKER

You're gonna go on as you, alright, I hope you make it back. Joan, Cindy, say good luck to Joy.

*Joan Rivers and Cindy walk up.*

JOAN RIVERS

Wow. You look great. Good luck today.

CINDY

Wow. Good luck.

NEIL WALKER

That's her. That's how she is.

JOAN RIVERS

She should be in a skirt. She's got nice long legs. Show her legs. Good luck!

JOY

Joan Rivers wants me in a skirt, but I'm gonna wear pants.

NEIL WALKER

Do what you want to do. Come on, let's go upstairs.

*He leads her out of the dressing room.*

INT. ROTATING QVC STAGE – DAY

*Profiled silhouette, Neil and Joy speak in the dark right before she goes on.*

> NEIL WALKER
>
> Are you nervous?

> JOY
>
> Yes.

> NEIL WALKER
>
> Just be yourself. Remember it's all in the hands. Here we go.

*Neil leaves. Joy remains, nervously holding the mop as the stage now rotates and rotates bringing her into the bright light, she continues to wait.*

> STAGE HAND
> (*off-screen*)
>
> Ready and, stage is moving, Household product 375 in three, two –

*A bell sounds. Then silence.*

INT. ROTATING QVC STAGE – DAY

*Joy's Christmas kitchen set rotates into super bright lights and stops. Joy is blinded staring into white lights, she can only barely make out the shapes of the cameras.*

*Neil watches her from near the cameras.*

> NEIL WALKER
>
> What are you doing? Come on, go! Go!

INT. JOY'S HOUSE – CONTINUOUS

*Rudy, Trudy, Mimi, Terry, Christy, Tommy, Jackie, Jackie's husband, Andre, watch.*

> TRUDY
>
> She's freezing.

INT. SOUNDSTAGE – CONTINUOUS

> JOY

Sorry these lights are so bright. Nobody tells you how bright these lights. Well, Neil did tell me. Neil is my boss here. I should thank him for letting me be up here.

> NEIL WALKER

You're Joy! Just say something. Talk about the mop. Oh my God. We have to do something, do we have a call? Can we go to a call? Is it a friendly call?

> STAGE MANAGER

It's a friendly call.

> NEIL WALKER
> (to Stage Manager)

Okay. Take it. Take it.

> NEIL WALKER
> (shouts to Joy)

Joy, we have a call!

> JOY

A call? How did that happen? We have a call.

> CALLER I

Hi, Joanne from New York.

> NEIL WALKER

Joanne from New York.

> JOY

We have a call coming in from Joanne from New York.

> CALLER I

I'm calling in because I'd love a mop that I don't have to touch when I wring it.

Cut to:


INT. JOY'S HOUSE

> JACKIE

You know my hands get raw when I mop broken glass and I wring the mop? I cut my hands.

97

*Back to Joy's face relaxing into a quiet smile, as she realizes it is Jackie.*

> JACKIE
> (*off-screen, on speaker*)
> Do you ever cut your hands when you're wringing?

> JOY
>
> Joanne, that is so funny that you said that. That is exactly how I was inspired to invent this mop. There was glass shattered everywhere. I was with my two kids with my father and every time I would wring the mop, I would get glass shards in my hands and the old mop just wasn't very absorbent, so I went to my daughter's room and I borrowed her crayons and I designed this mop. It's extremely absorbent with 300 continuous cotton loops that I looped myself when I designed it. It's made of plastic so it's lightweight but also very durable.

> NEIL WALKER
>
> Household item 375.

> JOY
>
> Household item 375. I guarantee you you're not going to find another mop like this that exists. If there was, I would have bought it, and I wouldn't have cut my hands up. You can get across the whole kitchen with one wring. Just imagine that. Chocolate syrup.

> NEIL WALKER
> (*to Camera Operator*)
> Go to the syrup. Go to the syrup.

> JOY
>
> And here's baby food, a very big spill at my house, a very common spill for me. So you dunk it into the soapy water as you do with any of your other mops, but the only difference is I don't have to use my hands when I wring it. And I guarantee you there will be no regrets, no returns. I have been mopping for most of my life. Every single day.

> NEIL WALKER
> (*shouts to Joy*)
> Phones are ringing!

JOY

I cannot tell you how much this mop has changed my life. The phones are ringing. The phones are ringing. This is going to be the greatest mop to have around Christmas time when you have family over. I am a mother of two. There is just spill after spill. Family comes to town. You can mop your entire kitchen with one wring. Oh my God. 29,000. This is very special. I haven't even told you about my personal favorite feature, which is the removable mop head that I can put into the washing machine and it will come out clean as new.

NEIL WALKER

Keep going, Joy.

JOY
(*laughing*)
Oh my God, these numbers keep climbing. Thank you. This is the most absorbent mop on the market. It's lightweight. It's the only mop that you're ever gonna buy, the best mop you're ever gonna use. It is lightweight and durable and that is just me speaking from my experience as someone who mops their house every single day from my heart.

*Neil watches Joy's personality come through, her warmth and directness.*

NEIL WALKER

This woman's gonna be a whole new business. (*He looks at the counter.*) No way.

*Joy looks at the counter as sales pass 47,000. Buzzer sounds and Joy is overwhelmed with emotion about what has just happened.*

*She cups her hand over her mouth as the stage rotates her back out of the light into the darkness. She stands quietly mouthing 'Oh my God' to herself.*

*She turns to see Neil backstage, runs off the stage to hug him.*

JOY

Can you believe it?

*Neil laughs.*

Can you believe it, I thought for sure you were going to tell me your counting machine was broken.

NEIL WALKER

I listened to you, you were right.

JOY

I just can't believe that actually happened.

NEIL WALKER

I guess you can say we're friends in commerce.

JOY

Friends in commerce.

NEIL WALKER

Let's promise if one day, and that day may come, that we become adversaries in commerce, that we remain friends. Because that's a true friendship indeed.

JOY

Friends in commerce, I agree, let's shake on it.

'Sleigh Ride' by The Ronettes starts.

Cut to:


EXT. RUDY'S GARAGE, RED SIGN IS LIT UP – NIGHT

Snow falls. Christmas lights.

Cut to:


INT. HANGAR BEHIND RUDY'S GARAGE – NIGHT

Rudy dances with Trudy, beaming with happiness as The Ronettes continue to play. Joy dances with Mimi and Christy. Then Peggy dances with Rudy.

Mimi talks to Joy, Tony holds Tommy.


EXT. RUDY'S GARAGE – NIGHT

Joy greets Neil in front of the garage in front of the lit-up sign.


INT. RUDY'S GARAGE – NIGHT

Neil shakes Rudy's hand inside the office as Joy introduces Neil to the family and shows him the factory floor.

JOY

This is where the mops are put together. We've got ten looms
and then when they're completed, this is where the mop heads
are sewn.

NEIL WALKER

To be honest with you, I expected this factory to be much
bigger. Who makes your parts?

JOY

A factory out in California. It was cheaper and faster than any
place around here.

NEIL WALKER

Smart, but are they going to be able to stay on schedule?

JOY

Yes.

*The Ronettes, 'Sleigh Ride', continues.*

*Cut to:*


INT. QVC STAGE – NIGHT

*Joy – happy, more confidently – sells the mop for a second time.
Numbers roll on the counter. Neil walks the stage, exuberant.*

*Cut to:*

*Backstage control room.*

*Joy, happy, runs in to take a phone call waiting for her in a solitary
area. We see her lit from below.*

JOY

Thank you, right here. (*Picks up phone.*) Hello!

*She listens to the phone call, her smile fades. Now the Ronettes are
gone, and a muted, soulful, percussive, acoustic guitar begins.*


EXT. JOY'S HOUSE – NIGHT

*Christmas lights on picket fence.*

*Joy walks, emotional, from car, through old gate to yard, scoops up
Christy, who runs to her from the house. She carries Christy in her
arms into the house. Guitar song becomes full acoustic chords: 'Angie'.*

INT. JOY'S HOUSE – CONTINUOUS

*Joy opens the door and walks in with Christy in her arms, to face: somber assembly of Terry, Rudy, Trudy, Peggy, Jackie, Eucaria, and Dr Whitten, all facing her silently. She has a moment of eye contact with each family member and friend.*

> DR WHITTEN
> She's not responding.

*Joy, pausing on stairs, looks back at everyone watching her silently.*

INT. MIMI'S ROOM – CONTINUOUS

*Joy, holding Christy, opens door – to see her beloved Mimi lying quietly, eyes closed, an IV attached to her arm.*

*Joy puts Christy down. Christy remains in the doorway as Joy walks to the bed, sits, looks down upon Mimi.*

> JOY
> (quietly)
> Mimi, Mimi.

*No response. Joy has a quiet moment of overwhelming emotion at the loss of her quietly strong grandmother.*

> GRANDMA MIMI
> (voice-over)
> I so hated to leave her that day. I had so much I wanted to say to her and to my great-granddaughter. I felt I wanted to stay near her.

EXT, ULTRA WIDE. WINTER CEMETERY – DAY

*Snow on the ground. Distant church bell. Joy, dressed in black, white flowers in her hands, places them carefully on the casket as she, Rudy and Trudy, take their folding chairs by the graveside. They sit in silence. Joy feels another hand in a glove grasp hers, she looks up to see Mimi, seated beside her, dressed in black. Mimi looks lovingly into Joy's eyes. A priest's bell turns Joy's eyes to look the other way. When she turns back, Mimi is gone – the chair is empty again. When Christy sits there, Joy kisses the top of her daughter's head.*

JOY
(*whispers*)

Christy.

*She then turns to face the service about to start. Everyone sits in silence. Rudy, seated next to Joy, leans over:*

RUDY
(*whispers*)

There's a problem in California.

JOY
(*whispers*)

There can't be a problem in California. I told Neil that everything was fine.

RUDY

Gerhart keeps raising his prices, he just did it again: more money per unit.

JOY

He can't do that. Were going to lose money.

RUDY

I sent a representative to handle him.

JOY

Representative? We don't have a representative. What representative?

RUDY

Peggy went.

JOY

Peggy?

*Rudy nods.*

I don't want to talk about this right now.

*A car door slams in distance. Joy looks over her shoulder to see Peggy walk from a taxi, across the snow, toward them, with the little blue suitcase in her hand.*

JOY

How could you send Peggy?

RUDY

She wanted to be a part of it. You both are blood relatives, you're half-sisters. It's very, very important that you love and respect each other.

*Cut to:*

INT. JOY'S HOUSE – NIGHT

*Mimi's room as a place of mourning, with candles beneath a framed photograph of Mimi, below which Joy sits, tense, facing her sister and father, also seated, all still dressed in mourning.*

PEGGY
(*quietly*)
I paid them the twenty that you owed them, I had to. I got them to fill the order of the 100,000, with the price increase of only two dollars per unit.

JOY
(*quietly*)
We can't increase at all, Peggy, don't you understand? We sold at a certain price, any hikes, especially the ones he's asking for, mean I will lose so much money that I'll be in even more debt than I was before.

PEGGY
You're gonna make it back.

JOY
I'm gonna make it back? How?

PEGGY
I've got ideas, you know. There are things that I like to do. I spoke to him about a project that Dad and I been designing. Right, Dad?

RUDY
Yes, we did.

*Joy is hurt and stung to hear this, but she contains it.*

JOY
Do you have any idea how much an idea will cost? How or where you'll sell it, if you can even manufacture it after it's

taken everything we've got to sell this one product that now
thanks to you is going to cost more money?

PEGGY

Maybe my product is better than your product.

*Joy's face flushes with withheld anger at this disrespect.*

I can do what you did on TV, it's not that hard. Isn't that the
whole purpose of that channel, that everybody can do it?

RUDY

What your sister does is not easy but what we were planning to
do is not that difficult.

JOY
(*quietly*)

Listen to me

*They stare at her.*

Never speak on my behalf, about my business again. Now I
have to go to California.

*Joy stares at Peggy.*


INT. CHRISTY'S ROOM – NIGHT

*Reflected in the bottom of an oval mirror: Joy leans down to kiss her
sleeping daughter goodbye as the incoming pre-lap of a jet engine
rumble begins.*

*Cut to:*


EXT. WHITE SKY LOOKING UP

*The underside of an airliner rumbles through the frame from below,
exiting top of frame.*

*Cut to:*


EXT. STREETS OF INDUSTRIAL LOS ANGELES – OVERCAST DAY

*Joy, in a ponytail and black jacket, looks at the map of the Thomas
Guide with one hand as she drives, alone, past the old aqueduct,*

*streets of warehouses, factories, mostly abandoned industrial streets.*

EXT. FABRI-PAC OLD BUILDING/FACTORY – CONTINUOUS

*Joy's small rental car stops, she gets out. Walks into the building.*

UNT. FABRI-PAC OLD BUILDING/FACTORY – CONTINUOUS

*Joy enters a seedy, small empty entrance foyer. An old standing sign with missing letters:* PLE SE ENTE *. An arrow points left.*

*Joy turns and opens the door to her left.*

INT. FABRI-PAC WAREHOUSE – STEPHAN'S OFFICE

*Joy's point of view: eerie, empty, old wall-to-wall faded blue carpeting, faded wood paneling, shabby office, with small radio playing an old pop song. An old metal desk. To her right, a glass case reads* PROUD PRODUCTS OWNED AND CREATED BY FABRI-PAC, *with Joy's mop inside the case. Joy's turns from the case, fierceness on her face.*

*A door opens behind the metal desk. A diminutive, eerie young guy in a navy blue hoodie enters.*

> EERIE YOUNG FABRI-PAC GUY
> (*off-screen*)
> Can I help you?

> JOY
> I'm Joy. I'm here to see Gerhart.

*He stares at her.*

> EERIE YOUNG FABRI-PAC GUY
> He's not available.

> JOY
> I'll wait.

*She stands her ground as we hear another man, Gregory, join the first, out of shot.*

> EERIE YOUNG FABRI-PAC GUY
> (*without breaking his gaze*)
> She said she's here to see Gerhart.

106

*The two guys stare.*

GREGORY OF FABRI-PAC

Gerhart. Gerhart.

*Joy continues to hold her ground facing these out-of-shot men. Fluorescent lights overhead flicker. A door opens behind Joy. She turns to see Gerhart walk in: tall, forty-five, unshaven, half-zipped hoodie.*

GERHART

Hey, I'm Gerhart.

*Joy turns and looks at Gerhart, a hard-looking man, forty, hair back.*

JOY

I'm Joy.

GERHART

Come on in.

*He turns and walks. Joy follows.*

INT. GERHART'S OFFICE – DAY

*Gerhart sits behind his desk in another wood-paneled room with a mounted fish on the wall behind him. Joy sits, facing him across the desk.*

GERHART

Derek Markham is my boss. He lives in Texas. Fabri-pac is one of several companies he owns or collects royalties for. I report to him. He makes pricing decisions.

JOY

I've never met or talked to this Derek Markham, but I've talked to you many times on the phone and I do find it very curious that the second I'm on television with a lot of success, the price for our products goes up. Seems very unfair to me to say the least. Seems like you're shaking us down.

*The large man enters the room, followed by the Eerie Guy.*

GERHART

You met Gregory, our plant foreman.

*Gregory looks at the documents with Gerhart.*

GREGORY

It's very hard to lower the cost at this point, we are already losing a lot of money.

JOY
(*evenly*)

How could that possible be with the 500,000 that we've given you? On top of the 50,000 of advance royalties that have gone to a Derek Markham in Dallas and that's not even counting what my sister paid you, without my authority by the way, for your overcharges and your mistakes.

GERHART

Your sister paid the increase that you refused to pay.

JOY

Well, she had no authority to do that, she's not an officer of my corporation.

GERHART

You can pay more.

JOY

I can't pay more. I won't.

GREGORY

Costs are higher. Wear and tear on the molds, we have to remake them every other week.

JOY

Is that so? Can I see the molds?

GERHART

They're in the machines, it'll take some time to prepare them for you.

*Tense pause.*

JOY

Is there a bathroom I can use?

*Gerhart scrutinizes her.*

GERHART

Sue, down the hall on the left. Gregory will show you.

*Gregory, who is very large, leads Joy down hall to bathroom.*

INT. BATHROOM – CONTINUOUS

> JOY

Thanks.

*She closes the bathroom door, leans against it, exhales frustration, tension, anger. She sees, across the bathroom, a pile of clutter – storage bins, tools, assorted things, in front of a storage door with safety glass four feet high.*

*She decides to try something. Criminally, stealthily, 'Stray Cat Blues' starts as Joy looks over her shoulder to be sure no one is looking as she begins the transgression she feels justified in doing –*

*Just outside bathroom door, Gregory waits for Joy to finish in the bathroom.*

*Back to:*

INT. BATHROOM – CONTINUOUS

*Joy clears the clutter that blocks the storage door, peers through the safety glass to see passageway to another room. She opens the small door, crouches through the space, hoping to find her injection molds, comes out the other side that leads her to –*

INT. INDUSTRIAL FLOOR – CONTINUOUS

*A large open industrial floor a hundred yards wide and long with a very high ceiling. Injection mold machines whir at the very far side, with operators moving equipment and products.*

*Joy looks around and walks toward tables with injection molds on them on this inactive side of the factory. She walks up to various tables. She sees blueprint designs to her mop open on a work table reading:* PROPERTY AND PATENT OF FABRI-CORP.

> JOY

What –

*She looks in shock at her stolen designs.*

> GERHART
> (off-screen, shouts)
> What are you doing in here?

(*shouts back*)
What is this? These are my designs. These are my molds.

GERHART
Those are ours, we knew you be trouble. The cops are on their way. We called them as soon as you showed up.

*Gerhart stands fifty feet away with four other men.*

JOY
These are my molds.

GERHART
Those are ours.

*Gerhart and the men walk toward her.*

JOY
I'm taking these with me. I'm taking all of these with me. I want all of these boxed up and I'm taking them.

GERHART
You're trespassing.

JOY
It's not your patent. These are my designs. I'm not going anywhere without my molds.

*Two Policemen walk toward her from far entrance of factory, as Gerhart and his men close in from the other direction.*

What! No. No. This is not stealing, this is my property. This is my property. I have all of these designs. These are all mine, they belong to me.

GERHART
She's from out of state, John. You've known me fifteen years.

*Joy stares at Gerhart and Gregory. Another man closes a large door leading to the outside. Joy walks toward the other door with rolled-up designs in her arms. She passes working machines and machinists.*

*The two Policemen walk in.*

POLICE OFFICER I
Alright, c'mon, ma'am. You're trespassing.

> JOY

What?

> POLICE OFFICER I

Yeah, c'mon.

> JOY

I'm not trespassing, I was in his office.

> POLICE OFFICER I

No. No. C'mon.

*'Stray Cat Blues' gets loud as the Policemen each take her by the upper arm and walk her toward the factory loading-dock steps. Joy looks back over her shoulder and shouts.*

> JOY

Gerhart, you're not going to get away with this. You're a thief, Gerhart, you're a thief.

> POLICE OFFICER I

Be careful what you're saying. Be careful. C'mon, stop.

> JOY

This is stealing.

> POLICE OFFICER I

Watch yourself.

*The Policemen walk her down the stairs to the police car where they cuff her hands behind her back as she first looks shocked, then protests wordlessly as they put her into the car.*

INT. TORRANCE JAIL CELL – DAY

*Jail bars slam shut on Joy. Song stops. She sits in cell behind bars.*

INT. LOS ANGELES HOTEL ROOM – DAY

*Joy sits behind desk listening, with Tony, to Ray Cagney, California Patent Attorney. Christy sits, with a toy toolkit, across the room with Tony.*

> RUDY

What about Trudy's money, Joy? You have to pay back Trudy's money. This is only getting worse.

TRUDY

I predicted tragedy, Joy. You're racking up quite a steep bill. We had to fly out here. Bail you out.

RUDY

Plus it cost us an extra 10,000 dollars for Ray Cagney, this California Patent Attorney, to get us to this point.

PATENT ATTORNEY RAY CAGNEY

We got the state to decline prosecution. They see it's a contract dispute. When you paid royalties to Derek Markham in Texas it puts all your part and molds under the umbrella of their patent. I see you brought all your drawings to prove your design. But it's impossible to fight it now. You were not properly advised.

*Joy's tension is pushed as Christy hammers her toy blocks.*

JOY

Christy, please. Tony, take her to bed.

CHRISTY

I don't want to go to bed, I want to stay here.

*Joy looks intensely at Rudy and Trudy.*

JOY
(to Rudy and Trudy)

I paid those royalties because you told me to. Because your lawyer told me to.

TRUDY

Our lawyer was mistaken. This happens sometimes in business. It didn't work out for you.

RUDY

It happens sometimes. Trudy's lawyer is not a patent attorney.

TONY

Which I said! And you said I had no business being Joy's advisor, and now it turns out that I was right.

TRUDY

That's not helpful now, Tony.

RUDY

That's enough, Tony.

TONY

Oh, it's enough now.

PATENT ATTORNEY RAY CAGNEY

I'm very sorry, I wish there was more I could do. But when your sister Peggy paid the unjustified bills that you refused to pay it closed the door on that.

JOY

What about Neil Walker and QVC? Wouldn't they pay the expenses on defending the patent?

RUDY

Be careful, Joy, you could be sued for misrepresentation and failure to deliver, that's breach.

TRUDY

QVC requires you to deliver a fully patented product.

PATENT ATTORNEY RAY CAGNEY

I've been doing this for a long time, you're in for a very long court process and you will probably lose. I wish I could do more.

RUDY

Thank you, Ray. You gonna have to accept the facts, Joy. You are almost half a million dollars in debt. I don't how you're going to pay it. We have to declare bankruptcy. You're gonna have to declare bankruptcy.

TRUDY

I have to declare bankruptcy.

RUDY

She has to.

TRUDY

To try to contain my losses. I have to write it off.

JOY

It just seems so wrong. We've worked so hard. We've come so far. For us to just give up now. It seems so unfair.

TRUDY

Business is unfair. That's it. It's not working out. Well, that's what happens. That's why people don't go around making inventions every other day. Wake up.

RUDY

It's my fault, I gave her the confidence to think she was more than just an unemployed housewife selling plastic kitchen stuff to other unemployed housewives on a junk cable channel. It's not your fault, honey. She pressured herself into doing something she shouldn't have done. It was wrong of us to put that pressure on you.

TRUDY
(shaking ice-cubes in glass)

I need more vodka. It was wrong of us to think that you'd be an instant business person overnight. Of course this is not who you are.

Trudy gets up and crosses the room. Gets in Joy's face and points.

TRUDY
(quiet and intense)

It takes a kind of toughness and a certain acumen that you simply don't have. Sign the paper.

Joy roils quietly inside at all of this, including Rudy's backhanded support.

RUDY

You have to sign these bankruptcy papers, honey. The notary's right outside. I'm going to get her.

Rudy escorts the Notary into the hotel room.

You're going to have to move out of your house immediately. You're going to have to move into an apartment – maybe you can move into a room in Trudy's house.

TRUDY

With her children?

RUDY

Yeah. You have room, she's my daughter, why not?

114

Let's talk about it.

*Joy stares at everyone in the room. Rudy handing her a pen.*

*Joy rises, emotionally drained and defeated, to sign the document. The Notary stamps it and leaves. Joy roiling.*

Thank you.

CHRISTY
Mimi said you're the one born to help carry the family to success.

JOY
(*irritably*)
No, Christy, Mimi was wrong. The world will not give you opportunities, the world will destroy your opportunities and break your heart. I should have listen to my mother when I was ten years old. I should have spent the rest of my life watching TV and hiding from the world like my mother. So I don't want to hear any more about Mimi. She was wrong, she had her head in the clouds and it was full of stupid ideas and it gave me stupid ideas. Like this, stupid, stupid idea.

*Joy turns picks up the metal prototype mop she first welded, brought to prove her case which is now lost, and smashes it against the wall. She attacks the wall where her original crayon design drawings are taped and tears them down in rage, her back to her family.*

CHRISTY
Mommy, don't tear them. No!

*Then she picks up a big stack of legal documents, raises them above her head, and throws them to the floor in disgust. She turns around out of breath and stares at her shocked, hurt family.*

JOY
Christy, I'm so sorry. I'm so sorry. Please go to bed. Everybody just go to bed.

CHRISTY
Goodnight, Mommy.

JOY
Goodnight, Christy, just go to bed.

I'm so sorry, Joy, I'm so sorry.

*Everyone leaves. It's quiet.*

JOY

Just go.

*She stands alone in the room, surveys the torn crayon design drawings all over the floor, and slowly pulls on the last shred of a drawing taped to the wall.*

*Cut to:*


INT. HOTEL BATHROOM – LATER

*Hair down from her ponytail, Joy stares at herself in the mirror, now the quiet, no-nonsense, unanxious presence in the room. And slowly raises her scissors and cuts her hair short, in some inner declaration of war and determination. Chop, chop, she cuts her hair length in half, and drops the scissors to the counter.*


INT. ADJOINING HOTEL ROOM – NIGHT

*Joy sits in the middle of the floor with her reading glasses on, reads through the many legal patent documents all around her on the floor.*

*Close on:*

*Papers joy is reading: legal documents – patents – design drawings for mops – Hong Kong documents – Texas Corporation documents – California documents —*


INT. HOTEL ROOM – MORNING

*Tony wakes up in his clothes on top of the covers of the king bed with the kids. Morning light fills the room. Half asleep, Tony looks at the sleeping kids. No Joy.*

TONY

Joy? Joy?

*He walks to the adjoining living room, sees it is empty, documents all over the floor. He sees a note taped to the mirror and reads it. As music begins.*

EXT. DALLAS STREET – DAY

*Joy in her black coat, pants, sunglasses, walks, unhurried, intense, on her mission, down pre-war street in Dallas. Christmas tinsel and lights along the street through different pools of music.*

*Joy crosses the street diagonally.*

EXT. DALLAS STREET/INT. PRE-WAR HOTEL

*Joy walks into the lobby of a pre-war hotel.*

INT. PRE-WAR HOTEL – LOBBY

*A small lobby. She passes the front desk clerk on her way to the old carpeted wooden staircase.*

*Upstairs, Joy opens the hotel room with the key. Inside:*

INT. PRE-WAR HOTEL – JOY'S ROOM

*She looks at the spare, Edward Hopper-esque room. She goes to the window, looks outside for someone arriving. wide shot from outside from a higher window, a solitary figure in the window. Back inside the room, she stares out the window.*

*A sharp knock on the door. She turns, surprised.*

JOY

It's open.

*Cut to:*

*POV: outside the door, over Dallas man's shoulder as he opens the door, A western suitcoat with a yoke, a white straw cowboy hat.*

*We see over his shoulder to Joy across the room by the window as she points back to him:*

JOY

You can leave the door open.

*The Dallas Man walks in, starts across the room, as Joy begins to cross back toward the door. They stare each other down as they pass each other, each poker-faced.*

*The Dallas Man has a cold, hard look as he goes over to the window, then looks back over his shoulder at Joy. A bit awkwardly she rests*

117

*her elbow on the bureau by the open door, to seem more comfortable than she is.*

*She looks at him, doesn't say anything.*

DALLAS MAN
*(he stares at her)*
No one knows I'm here. You don't even know who I am. I could be Derek Markham or I might be someone Derek Markham sent to handle you. You have no case. Maybe people think you came to Dallas in despair to take your own life because you were in such deep financial trouble suddenly from your little venture.

*Joy stares back at him. Tense. Is she defeated or not?*

JOY
I made a phone call this morning to Hong Kong. It was three a.m. in California but it was three p.m. the following afternoon in Hong Kong. I always think it's amazing how time works like that.

*She walks over to the table by the window, and sits on it.*

And I was fortunate enough to get on the phone with a Mr. Christopher who I found to be very friendly, which was surprising because I really haven't found the gentleman in California to be very nice considering we're all in business together. I told Mr. Christopher that the reason I was calling was to discuss the differences and the designs of our products. I was surprised to hear that Mr. Christopher had no idea about all the mops we've sold and I've paid you over $50,000 in advance royalties on behalf of Mr. Christopher, blood money from my family, and my second mortgage. Turns out Mr. Christopher doesn't know anything about those royalties so –

*Warming to her topic, she sits at the table.*

– it seems we have a case of fraud and embezzlement. And as if that weren't bad enough, I also discovered in the paperwork that our mops actually don't bear any similarities. So I never did owe you any royalties for your patent. That's another case of fraud. My lawyers really could go after you but I told them give me a day to see if maybe, you might have made a mistake, that you would correct, given the chance.

*She sits back in repose on the little in the hardwood chair, watches the effect of her new found leverage on the man who almost stole her business rights from under her.*

*She says nothing as she sits looking at the standing man. He stares her down. She waits to see what he will do.*

DALLAS MAN
We'll pay you back all the royalties you paid us.

*Joy stares steadily without moving, says nothing.*

I'll give you twenty-five thousand on top of paying you back the fifty.

*Joy looks down, brushes her lap off, then looks out the window into the light outside.*

Okay. I'll give you fifty thousand on top of paying you back the fifty.

*Joy turns her unflinching gaze from the window back to the man across the room. She says nothing.*

Plus interest.

*Joy takes a folded piece of paper from her coat pocket, unfolds it on the table and takes out a pen.*

JOY
I want all of my molds back, I want you to sign this piece of paper saying you have no rights financially, I'm just going to add you said the fifty plus the fifty plus the interest. So I just want you to initial next to those two numbers as well.

*Dallas Man exhales defeat and frustration as he walks over, takes the pen, in back-lit wide shot, and begins to sign. Music begins.*


EXT. DALLAS STREET — DAY

*Music crests and releases as Joy steps out of the hotel and walks happily, confidently, a different person than before this day, a more powerful person.*

119

GRANDMA MIMI
(*voice-over*)

She put up with just about anything, until when she had to bring the hammer down. She brought the hammer down. You don't become a boss without learning how to do that.

INT. QVC TELEVISION STAGE – DAY

*From darkness stage rotates into the television lights. Joy stands, fifteen years later, forty-two or forty-three, hair up, dressed for QVC sales anniversary, light breaking across her as she stands still as she did the first time, scared, rotating into the lights to speak to people at home.*

GRANDMA MIMI
(*voice-over*)

She couldn't know what was to come. That she would go on to make another hundred record-setting patents: 'Skinny Velvet Hangers Make Neater Closets'. That's a big deal to a lot of people. A special hanging travel mirror. I mean, who thinks of things like that. Joy did, but she didn't know any of this would happen as she walked that day in Dallas.

*Back to:*

*Dallas street as Joy walks happily away from the hotel – that day*

*Nat King Cole introduces 'A House with Love in It' from an old recording that plays.*

NAT KING COLE

Yes, sir, tonight's the night that old Saint Nick makes his yearly visit to all the folks all over the world. There's fun and expectation in every house across the land, and speaking of houses what do you say we take a little look in on a this one –

*Joy walks up to a toy store window with a little old speaker outside from which Nat King Cole is playing.*

*She looks through the window of the toy store at a snowy landscape with a train set and Christmas ornaments. A train emerges from the mountain and goes round the tracks.*

*She looks into the store window, looks up when snow starts to fall on her, sees the little machine above. She then looks at the toys inside, and watches a happy, intact family inside the toy store. A little girl, two parents, look at a wagon and a doll. Laughing. Joy watches, removes her sunglasses, she is sad inside. She puts her sunglasses back on. Resumes walking to:*

NAT KING COLE

Now I'll admit what you see right now is just a small piece of the front of the house but for all you grown-ups and kiddies alike, this is the time of Santa's magic, so I think we can make it become a real house. Even a house with love in it. Mr. Santa Claus, can we have a little bit of snow please?

*Snow begins to fall on Joy from above, with a clicking sound. She looks up to see small old theatrical fake snow machines attached to the toy store above the windows.*

*Joy stares up into the fake snow, letting it fall upon her face from the little machines above.*

NAT KING COLE

Thank you, that's fine. Now let me see what it really looks like inside this house. See what I mean?

*Nat's song begins.*

'A house with love in it, is rich indeed, although there are a thousand things that house may need. The carpet may be old, the room so plain and bare, and yet it's beautiful somehow when love is living there. A house with love in it just seems to bloom as though the month of may were filling every room.'

*Joy removes her sunglasses as she looks, through the fake snow, into the toy store and sees a father with two daughters, ten and seven, looking at a sled. Joy watches, with memories good and bad and emotion in her eyes.*

'So darling true the years with all my heart I'll pray a house with love in it is where we'll stay.'

*From Joy staring through snow, camera now tilts up from snow in front of Joy's new large shingled house.*

121

EXT. JOY'S NEW HOUSE – DAY

NAT KING COLE
(*sings*)

'The rooms so plain and bare and yet it's beautiful somehow when love is living there.'

*Moving men move furniture from a Mayflower moving truck into the house.*

INT. JOY'S NEW HOUSE – DAY

*Camera moves in one shot through:*

INT. JOY'S NEW HOUSE – KITCHEN

*New large kitchen where Terry cooks with Toussaint as Danica in the soap opera is on the small countertop television set.*

DANICA

Danica will never deny the power of her truth.

GRANDMA MIMI
(*voice-over*)

She didn't know that one day she would move her family into a big beautiful home.

*Camera continues past moving boxes in kitchen. Nat King Cole hands off to piano piece as at open of film.*

INT. JOY'S NEW HOUSE

*Around hallway filled with moving boxes, into dining room, full of moving boxes, where Rudy, Trudy, Peggy sit among the boxes on chairs, waiting to see Joy, along with other people standing in the room, waiting.*

GRANDMA MIMI
(*voice-over*)

Joy continued to help Rudy, Trudy, and Peggy, even when they sued her wrongly for ownership in the company and lost. As Rudy got older, he made products that failed and that Joy paid for, as she continued to take care of him, and love him.

*Camera passes Rudy, Trudy, Peggy, all older. Rudy has gray hair, a beard, glasses. Trudy's hair is also gray, and Peggy has some gray.*

*Camera continues through a door, a darkened empty room full of boxes, through another door to a warmly lighted, empty and bare sitting room where –*

*Three middle-aged businessmen stand talking in their suits. One turns around, it is Neil Walker, older.*

> JACKIE
> (*to Neil*)
>
> She's talking to her children.

> NEIL WALKER
>
> Is Tony in there?

> JACKIE
>
> Yes, Tony's in there, her family is in there.

> GRANDMA MIMI
> (*voice-over*)
>
> Her ex-husband and her best friend would remain her steadfast advisors.

*As camera circles Jackie talking to Neil and pulls away from Neil, leaving him waiting staring after Jackie as she leaves him waiting with his hands in his pockets and the QVC lawyers.*

INT. JOY'S WALNUT-PANELED HOME OFFICE – CONTINUOUS

*Camera reveals Tommy, now eleven or twelve, walking up to kiss his mother goodnight. Only see Joy from the back, her hair up and in the white jacket she wore on the QVC stage.*

> JOY
>
> I love you.

> CHRISTY
>
> Goodnight, Mom.

> JOY
> (*kisses Tommy goodnight*)
>
> I love you.

*Christy, now seventeen or eighteen, long hair, mature face, steps forward as piano continues,*

CHRISTY
(*kisses Joy*)

Goodnight, Mom.

*Camera pans to reveal Tony, older, in a suit, still divorced, and now working for Joy, as he kisses Christy and Tommy goodnight.*

*Joy, forty-two or forty-three, smiles as she watches them from her chair behind the desk.*

*Cut to:*

*Doorway of her home office as:*

*A young couple walks in, the young woman, twenty-five, carries a small cardboard box.*

JOY

Hi.

YOUNG MEMPHIS WOMAN

Hi.

JOY

Welcome.

*Young Memphis Woman and Husband sit down opposite Joy, who sips tea from a white china cup and replaces into the saucer.*

What do you have?

YOUNG MEMPHIS WOMAN

A traveling clothes cleaner –

JOY

Let's see it – So you're from Memphis.

YOUNG MEMPHIS WOMAN

Yes, I am.

JOY

You work as a waitress.

YOUNG MEMPHIS WOMAN

Yes, ma'am.

*The woman presents her neatly designed prototype to Joy. Joy uses it on her coat sleeve.*

JOY

Let's see, you made this yourself?

YOUNG MEMPHIS WOMAN

Yes I did, ma'am.

JOY

I made my first invention myself too. I like this, it's a very good design.

YOUNG MEMPHIS WOMAN

Thank you.

JOY

Can you stay an extra day to meet with our designers?

*She studies the woman.*

No, because of your boss? What hotel are you staying in right now?

YOUNG MEMPHIS WOMAN

The Holiday Inn.

*Joy looks to the side and addresses Jackie.*

JOY

Holiday Inn, let's move them over to the Radisson, get them a suite there, you'll be more comfortable with your baby. I'll call your boss and get it taken care of, give you an extra day. So that tomorrow you can come in meet with the designers, and we'll take it step by step, right.

YOUNG MEMPHIS WOMAN

Thank you.

JOY

We'll work on your ideas, see if we can do something.

YOUNG MEMPHIS WOMAN
(*tears up, emotional*)

It means so much to me. Thank you so much.

JOY
(*folding up the device*)

I know what it feels like, I know what it feels like to be in that chair. We'll see you tomorrow, okay? And good luck.

125

Thank you, ma'am.

*She hands the prototype back to the woman.*

TONY

Thank you for coming.

JOY
*(whispers, warmly)*
Go get the next person, Tony.

TONY

Okay.

*Enter Jackie with Neil Walker.*

JACKIE

Neil.

*Neil Walker comes in, takes a seat across from Joy.*

NEIL WALKER
*(as he sits)*
You dressed up for the QVC anniversary. I'm sorry we have
legal issues to discuss.

JOY

So am I.

*Neil looks at her across her desk. They are both older.*

NEIL WALKER

Here we are.

JOY

Here we are. Adversaries in commerce.

NEIL WALKER

Adversaries in commerce, and friends.

JOY

Yeah, and friends.

NEIL WALKER

I'm gonna tell you something, but you didn't hear it from me.

I don't know who you are or what you're talking about.

NEIL WALKER

I was hoping you'd say that. Barry's going to come after you hard, but that's just business, that's the way Barry is, he's a negotiator. Ultimately he needs you, he's buying HSN. It's all about HSN now, and he wants you to come with him. He needs you, you're gonna be very big over there. That's what's gonna happen. But you didn't hear it from me, right?

JOY

No, I sure didn't. But thank you.

*Neil looks at her and smiles warmly.*

NEIL WALKER

It's good to see you.

JOY

It's good to see you.

*They sit in silent communion and stare at each other.*

I'll see you around, pal.

NEIL WALKER

Yeah.

*He stands. Joy watches him go to the door. Neil pauses at the closed door and turns back to her.*

It's been a long journey.

JOY

Yes, it has.

NEIL WALKER

I'm proud of you.

*He looks back warmly as he opens the door.*

JOY

Thank you, Neil.

*He leaves, closes the door.*

*Joy is alone. She stares at the door thinking what a journey indeed it has been. She turns to profile, exhales with emotion. She looks down at the boxes all around her behind the desk, and bunch of piled books and things from the move.*

*Camera shows her hand as she reaches down, moves a couple of items, to reveal a faded old shoebox. When she lifts the lid, it is the box of paper creations from her childhood.*

*Prokofiev's 'Cinderella', which Young Joy played on her record player as a child, begins to play.*

*Joy reaches down and lifts the faded paper picket fence she made when she was ten and holds it delicately in her hands.*

*We hear the voices of ten-year-old Joy, as we saw at the start of the movie.*

TEN-YEAR-OLD JOY
*(voice, off-screen)*

This right here, this is a special power.

*Cut to:*

*Replay of Young Joy's hand in the air as it holds the paper bird she created at that time, as seen at start of film.*

This is a special power.

*Back to:*

*Joy's hands in the office now, as she places the paper picket fence back into the box, and picks up the paper fir tree we saw in her childhood. We hear replay of the young voice saying what she said at the start in her room as she played with her created paper world.*

And then I started to build my very own house, where I would live and make wonderful creations for all the world to see and have.

*Cut to:*

*Ten-year-old Joy holds the paper fir tree in front of her face.*

*Cut to:*

*Forty-three-year-old Joy holds the same paper fir tree in front of her face.*

128

*As Joy stares at the paper fir tree, her eyes go from memory to warmth and a hint of a smile breaks across her face.*

*A cappella opening of Cream's 'I Feel Free' starts again.*

*Joy lowers the little paper fir tree, and turns to look up.*

*Cut back to:*

EXT. DALLAS STREET

*As Joy walks from pre-war hotel – when she was twenty-eight that day.*

*She walks directly toward camera for several moments, looking directly into the lens. Then she puts her sunglasses back on, keeps walking directly to camera, and smiles.*

*Cut to:*

# JOY

*White letters over black.*

*End title and credits.*

# Joy

PHOTOS

,